"I'll be your matchmaker…"

Hannah held out her hand, waiting for Jake's handshake to seal their arrangement.

"Well, I…I don't know… It seems mighty strange…" He stood, pulling on the golden-brown beard that still did, in a way, link him with Lily.

"Jake, you know I'm the perfect person to do this for you. Who knows you better than me?" she asked, her hand still poised in the air.

He let out a long sigh. "Agreed." He clasped her hand lightly. "I guess."

"Uh-uh, Jake." She scolded him mildly. "This has to be what you want."

"All right, then…" He said the words tentatively, as if still testing the idea. "I agree."

"*Gut.* I'll start tomorrow, then." She began gathering up her canvas sacks, putting on her wool cloak.

"What? So soon?" His face clouded with unease, his eyes wide with—fear?

She'd rarely ever seen her friend appear afraid. The sight of him looking that way stirred her heart.

"It's going to be all right, Jake," she said softly, placing a comforting hand on his arm. "You'll see. Have I ever let you down?"

Cathy Liggett is an Ohio girl who never dreamed her writing journey would take her across the world and to Amish country, too. But she's learned God's plans for our lives are greater and more creative than the ones we often imagine for ourselves. That includes meeting her husband at a high school reunion and marrying three months later—nearly forty years ago. Together, they enjoy visiting kids and grandkids and spoiling their pup, Chaz.

Books by Cathy Liggett

Love Inspired

Her Secret Amish Match

Visit the Author Profile page at LoveInspired.com.

Her Secret Amish Match

Cathy Liggett

LOVE INSPIRED

INSPIRATIONAL ROMANCE

Recycling programs
for this product may
not exist in your area.

ISBN-13: 978-1-335-56737-6

Her Secret Amish Match

This edition published by arrangement with Harlequin Books S.A.

For questions and comments about the quality of this book, please contact us at CustomerService@Harlequin.com.

Love Inspired
22 Adelaide St. West, 40th Floor
Toronto, Ontario M5H 4E3, Canada
www.LoveInspired.com

Printed in U.S.A.

A new heart also will I give you,
and a new spirit will I put within you:
and I will take away the stony heart
out of your flesh,
and I will give you an heart of flesh.
—*Ezekiel* 36:26

To my incredible husband,
best friend and forever love.
Who would've ever imagined nearly forty years ago
that we would've found each other again?
I've got to say, I'm truly thankful that God
is the best matchmaker of all!

Chapter One

❧

"I got the mail for you, *Daed.*"

Wrench in hand, Jake Burkholder looked up from the plow he was intent on fixing and saw his daughter Sarah standing close by, holding a handful of envelopes.

A slight breeze whispered through the open doors of the barn, causing wisps of hair to escape from her *kapp*. With her free hand, she pushed away the dark brown curly strands, revealing wide, blue-as-sky eyes that resembled her mother's. Even though nearly two years had passed since his wife, Lily, had gone to the Lord, there were moments when their daughter's similar gaze caught him off guard.

The children had spent the sunny Saturday morning gathering eggs and helping with other daily chores. After that, while he focused on his repair work, Sarah and the twins settled on the straw floor of the barn, hovering over the new litter of playful calico kittens.

At least, he'd thought that was what they were doing.

But apparently, Sarah had made her way down their stretch of driveway to the mailbox at the side of the country road that curved in front of their house. She'd also made her way back up the driveway without him even noticing her disappearance. Not that a trip to the mailbox in their part of Sugarcreek, Ohio, was anything close to perilous. But it did concern him to think he'd been so preoccupied with his work that he hadn't even realized she'd been gone.

"*Danke*, Sarah." He took the mail, stuffing the envelopes into the pocket of his black pants. "But next time, you must ask if you may go down to the mailbox."

The oldest of the children, Sarah was close to turning six years old. Yet ever since Lily had been gone, he could tell she had been trying to take on her mother's role as much as she could. Her willing heart, ready to assume extra responsibilities, touched him. And tore at him, too.

He hated to reprimand her for being helpful. Yet, as her father, he needed to be ever protective of her physical safety. That went for his four-year-old twins, too, who were looking up from the pile of kittens. "Do you understand, Sarah?"

"*Jah, Daed.* I do." She nodded solemnly. At the same instant she spoke, her stomach growled, causing them both to smile.

"It sounds as if there's a tiger inside you that would like to be fed," Jake teased. "Are you *hungrich*?"

"I'm hungry!" Eli answered before Sarah could get a word out.

"Me, too," Clara, Eli's twin, chimed in.

"I suppose it is close to mealtime," Jake agreed. Actually, he realized guiltily, since the mail had already arrived, that meant it was hours past their usual noon meal. He'd not only lost track of Sarah, he had totally lost track of time, as well.

"I can make peanut butter and jelly sandwiches for us, *Daed*," Sarah quickly offered.

He was almost tempted to let Sarah take charge. He hated to break away from his maintenance work, not knowing when he'd get back to it. Plus, there was a fence that needed mending. Horse stalls to be cleaned. And those were only two chores on a never-ending list. Pausing, he considered his options but quickly came to realize what he already knew. Children required their own kind of maintenance, and that was especially true when they were missing a mother's attention and love.

"*Nee*, Sarah. Let's go in and eat together."

While he put his tools away, Sarah gathered up the twins like the mother hen she was. Jake smiled at the way she cautioned them in the same manner he'd spoken to her.

"Eli and Clara, did you hear what *Daed* said before? Don't go to the mailbox without asking." Sarah paused to wag a finger at her siblings.

"Oll recht," Clara replied, and Eli gave a quick nod.

With that, the three of them scampered ahead of him down the walk toward the house.

After the dimness of the barn, Jake couldn't help but be struck by the brightness of the autumn day. Glancing at his surroundings—the golden colors of the changing leaves and the vibrant blooms on the chrysanthemums—he felt a surge of gratitude that he was able to move into the home he'd grown up in after Lily's passing. His younger brother, Samuel, had had his fill of caring for the property their parents had left to them, and had readily taken off with a friend to Kentucky and new opportunities.

Jake was also thankful for the ridge of pine trees that separated his family's property from the Keims' land. All year long, those towering trees blocked the view of the house where he and Lily had been raising their family. But unfortunately, neither a row of trees nor anything else could block out the haunting memories of his and Lily's years together in that house.

Of course, it wasn't like he hadn't known their marriage was starting out with a lie. As it turned out, their marriage had ended with lies, too.

Jake felt relieved that Lily's brother, David, had put their family's property on the market soon after her death. Two years later, Jake wondered if potential buyers could feel a sadness still lingering in the walls.

As for the walls and rooms and land that now surrounded his children, he hoped to build as many happy memories as he could.

Just not with any indoor pets.

"Eli, leave the kitten outdoors," he called to his son, whose right pants pocket bulged with the furry creature he'd hidden there. Obviously, Eli hadn't thought he would notice, causing Jake to smile. Caring for three *kinner* surely kept him on his toes and was often overwhelming. Just keeping watch over his son was a job in itself.

For sure it would be good when his sister Esther, now all grown up herself and a teacher, arrived from Lancaster County to help with his children as she'd promised. As it was, every time he had a nanny from the community whom he thought would be a keeper, something would happen to pull them away and leave him stranded again.

Of course, Esther had made the same promise before and hadn't come through. He shook his head at the thought, not even wanting to consider the possibility of her changing her mind.

"Should we put Eli's kitten back in the barn with the others?" Sarah asked.

"That would be a very *gut* idea."

While the children took off on their mission back to the barn, Jake continued on his way to the house. He was almost to the front door when he heard the faint clip-clop of horse hooves. Immediately his trio of *kinner* broke out into a chorus of squeals.

"Hannah! Hannah!"

Jake turned to see Hannah Miller's spotted horse and buggy coming up the drive. The sight of Hannah always gave him much relief.

For months following Lily's passing, many kind people had brought meals, advised on child-care and tried to help in his new life as a single parent. But as time went on, they'd fallen to the wayside. Without any members of his family— or Lily's—living close by, there was no one consistent in his life or his children's. Except for Hannah.

Deftly hitching her horse to a post, Hannah gracefully stepped down from the buggy. Seeing her brought about a reaction in him just as when they were *youngies*. Back then, her chestnut-colored hair reminded him of milk chocolate, and her hazel eyes with their golden tint like fireflies lighting up on a summer's night. In a way, they still did.

He noticed hugging the *kinner* was Hannah's first order of business. The second was to unload the canvas sacks she'd brought. The children practically tripped over themselves, eager to help carry something into the house, each looking so happy to see her.

"Hannah, this is a *gut* surprise," he said, catching up with them. "Let me help." He reached for the covered pie dish in her arms, catching a whiff of it as he did.

"Cherry?" he asked.

"The *kinner*'s favorite. I was making a pie for worship at the Lapps' tomorrow, and I thought, why not bake two?"

Jake nodded. "Because managing Sew Easy and having your disabled aunt living with you isn't enough work for you, *jah*?" "How is your *aenti* Ruth, by the way?"

Hannah smiled. "Very *gut*, *danke*. As you know, she hasn't had use of her legs since birth and has been in a wheelchair all her life, but she can still run circles around me when it comes to most things."

"You know, you do need to take time to do things for yourself sometimes, Hannah."

"I am doing something for myself." She looked from him to his children. "I'm visiting my three favorite *kinner* in the whole wide world," she announced, causing the children to jump up and down with excitement.

"Daed," Sarah spoke up right away. "May Hannah eat lunch with us?"

"You're just now having lunch?" Hannah grinned at him curiously. "It's kind of late, don't you think? Closer to suppertime."

"Jah, we got a bit off schedule today."

"Daed's been working on the plow," Clara informed Hannah.

"Oh, I can see how a person could lose themselves in such an interesting project." Hannah's eyes glimmered as she teased. "Sounds real fascinating."

"Verra." Jake smiled back. "So, will you stay and eat with us?" He hoped she would stay awhile for the children's sake. And, honestly, for his sake, too.

"Ah. Well, I was just going to drop by with new dresses I'm stitching for the girls. I don't want you going to any trouble cooking for me."

"Please stay," Eli pleaded, and his sisters chimed in.

"We could have an early supper," Jake said, hoping to persuade her.

Hannah looked from his eyes to each of the

children's faces. "I'd love to stay. An early supper sounds perfect."

After depositing the canvas sacks in the catch-all room that also housed a sewing machine, they walked into the kitchen. The messy countertops and stacks of dirty dishes piled in the sink made Jake feel somewhat self-conscious. But Hannah said nothing. Instead, she started to wash her hands, obviously ready to help with the meal.

"Nee." Jake shook his head and pointed toward a kitchen chair.

"Have a seat and rest while we make the food."

The children were accustomed to helping him in the kitchen as best they could each day, but cooking for Hannah put a different spin on things. Jake noticed that suddenly they appeared far more earnest about their tasks. Eli squeezed the lemons mercilessly to get every drop of juice from them, only stopping when he needed to rest his arm from the workout. Sarah and Clara got busy deciding on the very best vegetable bowls and serving spoons, as if their lives depended on it.

Of course, they beamed when Hannah noticed their efforts. "Sarah and Clara, you do good work," Hannah complimented them. "And, Eli, you look as if you're a natural in the kitchen, just like your *daed.*"

That comment drew a chuckle from Jake. "Oh, *jah*. I'm a natural, all right."

"You cook real *gut, Daed*," Sarah defended him.

"I'm only teasing your father, Sarah, because he wreaked havoc in a neighbor's kitchen when we were much younger."

"What happened, *Daed*?" Sarah's eyes widened. Eli and Clara glanced up from their tasks, looking concerned, too.

"One of the neighbors, Mrs. Fisher, was teaching your *mamm* and Hannah how to can tomatoes," he started to explain. "I'd gotten done with my chores early and—"

Hannah smiled. "He thought he might want to learn, too. But, oh, he made such a mess with the tomatoes."

"I did, didn't I?" He laughed at the memory. "I accidentally broke a few mason jars, too."

"*Jah*, indeed. Mrs. Fisher shooed you out of the kitchen and sent you into town to buy more jars."

"Poor woman. She was nice about it, too," he said. "Even though I'd tested her patience." He shook his head. "Well, I've gotten somewhat better around the kitchen since then."

He'd had to. But he didn't want to think about the reason why at that moment. The children were in a cheerful mood and he was, as well. He was glad when Hannah diverted the conversation.

"How about if I at least set the table?"

"That's fair. Girls, can you help Hannah find everything?"

The girls instantly went to work with Hannah, who also oversaw Eli as he shakily carried his very full pitcher of lemonade to the table. Jake completed the meal with bowls of vegetables and a platter of leftover chicken.

As they all sat down, he looked around the oak table, taking note of the children's content faces and Hannah's serene expression. It felt somewhat strange, as it always did when Hannah visited, to look up and see her sitting at the table in Lily's seat. But after the past two years, he realized it was beginning to feel more comforting than strange. Hannah's company and spirit were truly a salve they all needed.

"Let us have a prayer yet," he said, then watched his children fold their hands together properly before he bowed his head and closed his eyes. Without a doubt, he was always ready to give thanks for *Gott*'s multitude of blessings. But on this day, at this moment, he felt moved to express his extreme thankfulness in a way he hadn't done in a long while.

After everyone helped clear the table and Jake coaxed little Eli into helping with the dishes, Hannah took Sarah and Clara to the extra room down the hallway.

Early-evening sunlight poured in the window, streaking across the girls' grinning faces, making it easy for Hannah to see how excited they were about their new dresses. To be able to do such a thing for her best friends' children tugged at her heart in a bittersweet way.

Thankfully she hadn't put off bringing the sample dresses for the girls—especially where Sarah was concerned. Hannah noticed the close-fitting dress she wore. She'd grown even more than Hannah had realized.

As both girls stood next to each other, Hannah slid the dresses over their heads. Clara's fit perfectly, but she'd misjudged Sarah's size. The new dress was as snug as her old one. But instead of focusing on the uncomfortable fit, Sarah looked up at her with the widest smile. "This is a real pretty green color."

"I thought it would go well with your hair and eyes, Sarah."

"What color goes with me?" Clara asked.

Clara's coloring was just like her mother's and father's, blonde with electric blue eyes. "I like blue on you, little one," Hannah told her. "But I have lots of fabric of other pretty colors, too. Once I get them all sewn, both of you girls will have plenty of warm dresses for the colder weather."

She stepped back and eyed them both once

more. "Clara, your dress fits well. But give me a minute to place some pins for new seams, Sarah."

As she knelt on the ground in front of Jake's oldest, pinning the garment, Clara leaned up against her side.

"You like to sew, don't you?"

"*Jah*, dear girl, I do. I've been doing it since I was a young girl."

When Jake moved into his parents' old house, she'd been happy to see that he'd brought along the treadle sewing machine that had once belonged to Lily's grandmother. When Lily's parents, Noah and Rachel, kindly took her into their home after she lost her family at ten years old, Hannah had felt comforted to see the machine in the Keim household. Certainly, sewing had reminded her of her own *mamm* in a lasting, heartfelt way like nothing else did. She'd taken to the craft, making it her life's work.

For the past seven years, her job at Grace Newberry's Sew Easy shop had never been just a means to keep her and her aunt fed and to pay her bills. It was the very desire of her heart. She loved helping the customers. She loved teaching and being creative. The *Englisch* store owner had promised that the shop would be hers one day soon when Grace retired, which was far more than she could ever have hoped for. It was the perfect answer for her. Because knowing what it felt like to be orphaned, she never wanted to feel that way again. She yearned to be self-sufficient and not depend on anyone but herself.

"Will you teach me how to sew?" Sarah spoke up.

"*Jah*, I would love to teach you."

"Me, too?" Clara asked.

"*Jah*, you, too." Their interest warmed her heart. "I'd enjoy giving you both lessons if it's okay with your *daed*."

After Hannah resized the last of Sarah's seams, the girls helped her gather up the basted dresses and turn off lanterns. Then, skipping down the hall ahead of her, they rushed to tell their father their news.

"Hannah is going to give us sewing lessons, *Daed*," they announced gleefully.

Hannah also heard their father's reply. "That's nice, girls," he said, but his voice was alarmingly flat. Completely different from the cheerful way he'd acted an hour earlier. His reaction quickened Hannah's feet till she reached the family room, too. In the amber glow of the lamp sitting on the table next to him, she could see his stricken face. She could also see an envelope and a crumpled piece of stationery on top of the table.

"Jake, is everything all—"

"Girls," he cut her off, getting up out of the chair, "your *bruder* is getting ready for bed. Go do the same." He pointed to the staircase. "I'll be up to say prayers when you're ready."

Without another word, he stepped over to the window, staring into the darkening sky. The girls glanced at her, clearly puzzled. She couldn't help but feel the same way. She tried not to let it show.

"Good night, sweet *maedels*." She gave the pair a wink.

Ever obedient, the girls did as they were told. Not until they were up the stairs did Jake turn and look at her. There was no denying he was completely beside himself.

"Jake, what happened?"

He ruffled a hand through his blond hair. "It's Esther."

"Is your sister *oll recht*?"

"*Jah*, she's just fine. But once again, she's broken her promise to me. She says they haven't been able to find a replacement for her at her school, and she cannot leave her teaching position to come help her nieces and nephew. Can't come to help her own flesh and blood."

Hannah wanted to reach out and calm him, but he began pacing. It was heartbreaking to see the defeated slump of his broad shoulders and the darkness in his usually smiling, warm blue eyes. This was the man who had always been so confident and sure of himself, the good-looking boy that all the girls crushed on and all the other boys wanted to be like.

"Jake, I'm sure she didn't mean it like that exactly."

"It doesn't matter how she meant it. The point is, she's not coming."

Hannah didn't bother to ask about other family members in Lancaster who might be able to come to Ohio to help. They'd covered that ground before. Whereas Esther was better acquainted with all their aunts and uncles and cousins since she'd spent the first ten years of her life there, Jake had been only two years old when his parents had moved from Pennsylvania to Ohio. Plus, from what his sister had written, those distant relatives were busy with their own lives and families.

"Oh, Jake, I'm sorry it's not working out like you hoped."

"*Jah*, well…" He stopped pacing and shook his head, sounding half-angry and completely distraught as he spoke. "I really needed her help. I can't provide for my *kinner* and also watch over them. It's a problem I can't seem to solve. But what else is new?"

"You know, Jake…" She hesitated. "Maybe a nanny isn't the answer you're looking for."

His brows arched, all six feet of him stiffening. "Oh, *jah*, while I'm out in the fields working, I'll just have the mares watch the *kinner*," he said curtly.

"What I mean is, a nanny can be a temporary solution. But it's not a permanent one."

"Hannah, you're confusing me."

She was sure he'd forgotten that when some townsfolk spoke of her, they said she had a special gift. Namely, the way she matched a man and a woman together. She was thrilled to help others find love. It took the pressure off finding her own match while keeping her heart intact and not being hurt again. More like devastated, as she had been by the unaware man she was looking at.

Yet she'd never mentioned matchmaking to Jake before, knowing he was still getting his bearings after Lily's death two years earlier. She also knew, however, that the once most popular boy in their community had become a solitary man out of necessity and his chances of crossing paths with a mate were slim. So, she was happy to try to find him a match, if he was willing.

"Jake, I think your *kinner* need so much more than what you can pay a stranger to give them." From her own background, she knew that better than anyone. "They need a nurturing female who is always there for them. And always there for you, their *daed*. Someone who knows you all well and cares for all of you, too."

"And you're saying what?" His forehead pinched.

"What I'm saying is, I can help you find that someone. But let me tell you, Jake, it means you'll have to start dating."

"Dating?" His jaw slacked.

"Well, *jah*. How else do you think you can find a mate?"

"To be honest, I've been so busy working and raising the children, I've not thought about finding a new wife."

"Well, what do you say, then? I'll be your *verra* own matchmaker. Agreed?" She held out her hand, waiting for his handshake to seal their arrangement.

"I… I don't know… It seems mighty strange…" He stood, pulling on the gold-tinted beard that had and still did link him with Lily. Then he began shaking his head nonstop. She wasn't sure if he was declining her offer or couldn't believe the offer she was making. "So, then I'd be just like one of the other Sugarcreek couples that you've brought together?"

"You mean like the other happy Sugarcreek couples that I've successfully matched? Yes, Jake," she answered reassuringly.

He eyed her warily.

"Jake, who knows you better than me? I'm the perfect person to do this for you." she said.

"Sure, but…" He let out a long sigh. Then finally, slow as a turtle poking its head out of its shell, his right hand came out of his pocket. Hesitantly, he reached for hers.

"Agreed." He clasped her hand lightly. "I guess."

"*Gut.* I'll start looking for a match tomorrow, then." She began gathering up her canvas sacks, then put on her warm cloak.

"Tomorrow? So soon?" His face clouded with unease, and his eyes seemed wide with—fear?

She'd rarely ever seen her friend appear afraid. Could barely recall a time even when they were younger that he'd seemed frightened. The sight of him looking that way stirred her heart. "It's going to be all right, Jake," she said softly, placing a comforting hand on his arm. "You'll see. Have I ever let you down?"

Chapter Two

The next morning was as drizzly and cloudy as Jake's thoughts while he steered his buggy over the damp, narrow roads through Sugarcreek. What in the world had he been thinking when he agreed to allow Hannah to find him a *fraa*? As if finding a new wife was as easy as buying a bale of hay at the feed and seed store. And what would the *kinner* think about him bringing another woman into their lives?

"Daed..." Sarah drew out the word as her concerned voice came from the back of the buggy, interrupting his thoughts.

His hands tightened on the reins. *"Jah*, Sarah?"

"Eli doesn't have any socks on."

"What? No socks?" Puzzled, he glanced over his shoulder at the boy, who was wedged between his sisters. "Eli, I thought you knew how to dress yourself by now, *sohn*. It's forty degrees outside."

"I didn't have clean ones, *Daed*." Eli folded his arms over his chest defensively. "All mine are muddy."

"That's silly." Clara reprimanded her twin, sounding much like her older sister. "If I can have on dirty clothing extra days, you can have on dirty socks, too."

Jake was at a loss for words. Didn't know what to say or think—except he needed to get the laundry under control. If that was even possible.

Oh, dear Lord, I need Your help, don't I?

Currently, however, socks, clothing and every other soiled item would have to wait. Before he headed his *kinner* back home to do more chores, he needed to put up more flyers around town, announcing his availability to do handyman work.

After Lily's passing, he'd left his job at the lumberyard to work the fields of his farm. He needed to be close to home and his children, even knowing full well—like his brother, Samuel— that farming wasn't what he was best suited for. It was also no mystery that the yield from farming was uncertain. Thankfully, *Gott* had made sure that the first harvest was plentiful, while he and the children were still grieving and finding their footing.

But this year, the harvest had been mediocre at best. As a result, he'd had to find other income. Though he'd already taken on a few handyman jobs, he hoped to pick up more work during the winter months ahead.

Turning those hopes over to *Gott*, he hitched the buggy in front of McNab's Hardware Store, and the children hopped out eagerly. Why wouldn't they? Kauffman's Kitchen was right next door and he'd promised them a late breakfast there. Not that the money he'd earned days earlier from his repair work was burning a hole in his pocket, by any means. But he figured the change of scenery and something other than his own cooking would do them all good.

It shouldn't have taken long to guide Sarah and the twins through McNab's, tack up a flyer and then head to Kauffman's. Yet, herding his family always took more time than he thought it should. A dropped glove here. A tripped toe there. It was at least twenty minutes before they were seated at a table and ordering their favorite foods.

The outing could've been relaxing except for Eli's elbow knocking over a glass of chocolate milk, then Clara dropping her fork on the floor. Jake leaned under the table to pick it up, then heard his name, raised his head too quickly, smacked his skull on the edge, and looked up to see Seth Hochstetler standing next to his chair.

Seth, his former employer and owner of Hochstetler's Lumberyard, smiled at him as if he could empathize. "It's not easy, *jah*? But I know you can handle whatever *Gott* throws at you."

Jake laughed, rubbing his head. "It's not always easy with these three."

"Just wait till they're teens." Seth seemed to be talking from experience as he nodded over his shoulder at his wife and their son and daughter seated several tables away. Jake also noticed Seth's younger sister Emma seated with them. "I'm glad I ran into you, Jake. Your name's been coming up, and I've been meaning to ask you something."

At that point, a smile lit up Emma's face as she looked over at Jake and gave a little wave. He tentatively waved back. He hoped Seth wasn't about to set him up with Emma. Did he seem that desperate and ill-equipped, sitting there with his children?

Glancing around the room, he looked for signs of spilled milk or utensils on the floor. But all he could see were families eating and enjoying themselves.

Yes, he probably did need all the help he could get from Hannah, Seth or whoever else. Realizing that, he looked at Seth, prepared to hear what his old boss had to say.

Hannah assumed it was the chilly rain keeping customers away from Sew Easy that afternoon. At least, she hoped the nasty weather was the cause and not the recent opening of the fabric chain store that people had been raving about.

So far, she'd waited on two older ladies, both only needing thread. Then, an hour or so later, the postman had arrived with several envelopes and parcels.

Her boss, Grace, had said she'd be busy with her retired husband for the rest of the day. Without her there to talk to, the store was virtually silent.

Normally, the solitude would've been boring. But all day Hannah's mind had been going a mile a minute, thinking about the prior evening and all that had happened with Jake.

As she stood at the counter methodically measuring remnants of material, rolling up the pieces and attaching a price tag, Hannah knew what she needed to do to get her thoughts in order. Closing her eyes, she bowed her head.

Dear Gott, *I'm forever grateful that You found a home for me as a child. One day if and when I'm ready, I may have You find a home for my heart, too. But right now, things aren't about me. As You know, I made a promise to Jake to find him a wife. But my words can only come true if You're there to help, Lord. So, I'm thanking You in advance for finding a woman who will love his* kinner *like I do—and the right person for Jake, too. In Your Son's name. Amen.*

She opened her eyes and sighed, immediately feeling more relaxed. It helped, too, when she spotted Anna Graber coming through the door. Rushing out from behind the counter, she hugged her friend, leaving enough room for Anna's protruding belly.

"Anna, how *gut* to see you! You look beautiful," she exclaimed truthfully. "When are you due?"

"Three months, and trust me, I'm not feeling anything close to beautiful." Anna grinned, massaging her round stomach. "But look at you, Hannah. So pretty, as always. When are you going to let a man snatch you up?"

Hannah felt the heat of a blush encircle her neck. After all, it wasn't like any men had been chasing her lately. And even if they had been, she wasn't much interested. After a few short-lived relationships, she'd realized she was far better at creating other people's happily-ever-afters than finding a match for herself. Plus, there was no wear and tear on her heart. The thing that really interested her right now was thinking about her future at Sew Easy. And as soon as she got Jake settled in a relationship, she could go back to concentrating on business.

"I've been so busy with work and teaching

sewing classes. Oh, and helping *Aenti* Ruth organize an embroidery class here." Knowing those things might not sound like good excuses, she added, "And I've been helping Jake with Sarah and the twins."

"How is Jake?" Anna tilted her head, looking concerned. "Matthew and I only have the two boys so far, but it's endless work. It's so nice of you to be there for him. I don't know how he does it alone."

"*Jah*, I know. That's why I promised to find him a match," she blurted out, without meaning to.

"You're his matchmaker?" Anna chuckled, her eyes growing wide. "Some things never change, huh? Remember when you and Lily tried to match me with Jake back when we were *youngies*?"

"How could I forget?" Hannah giggled. "We thought he should have a real girlfriend instead of always being with girl friends like Lily and me. And it might've worked if you had just shown up." She laughed again. When Anna didn't appear for their date, Jake had quickly brushed it off. Instead of being angry, he'd made them laugh, saying too bad for Hannah and Lily that they were stuck with him. On that day, he became everything she thought a boy should be.

"I couldn't. I was too shy back then," Anna admitted. "And Jake was the cutest *buwe* I'd ever seen." She shook her head. "Honestly, Hannah, I always thought you and Jake would end up together."

The words clutched at Hannah's heart, stealing her breath away. Still. After all this time. Because when it came to Jake, she'd simply been young and foolish. She'd taken his sweet words and smiles and turned them into big hopes for the future. And the time he held her hand in his before she left for Indiana to take care of her sick aunt? Well, she'd felt something she'd never felt before. But apparently, it had just been his way of saying goodbye. Because by the time she'd returned home with *Aenti* Ruth, he and Lily were about to be married.

She waved a hand at her well-meaning friend, much the same way as she shooed that past hurt from her mind and heart. "Jake and me? Oh, no, no. Jake and Lily were my best friends, you know that. Lily was like a sister to me." She paused. "I mean, I didn't see them as much after they were married. They were busy with their family. But whenever I stopped to count my blessings, I always counted my friendship with Lily and Jake twice. Now with Lily gone, well, I could never repay the kindness the Keims showered on me when I was a girl, but maybe I can help Jake and his children, you know?"

"It's a shame that Lily's *mamm* had a stroke right after Lily passed." Anna shook her head. "She was living with David up in Middlefield before that, wasn't she?"

"Yes, Rachel lived there ever since their *daed*, Noah, departed this world just shortly after Jake and Lily's wedding," Hannah replied.

"I remember him as a kind, soft-spoken man."

"That he was." Rachel Keim had never seemed thrilled with Hannah being in their home. But not so with Noah. All through their growing-up years, Noah and her father had been close friends and neighbors until they'd married and moved a couple of towns apart. When Noah heard she had lost her parents and two younger siblings in a tornado that crushed their home while she was at school one day, he had offered her a place in the Keim home. He treated her with love, like his own daughter.

Though it had hurt her immensely to have Noah leave this world, she'd found peace knowing he was with the Lord. "He was *verra* gentle and sweet."

"And so are you, Hannah." Anna placed an affectionate hand on her shoulder. "It's so kind of you to help with Rachel and Noah's grandchildren. And as for finding Jake a match…" She leaned closer. "I'm thinking you may have your first candidate right over there."

Anna turned her head and Hannah followed, their gazes landing on petite Rebecca Fisher at the front of the store. Barely visible from the bolts of material surrounding her, she'd slipped in quietly. Anna was right—on a list of possible brides-to-be for Jake, Rebecca was a definite prospect.

"I'm just looking around today, so don't worry about me," Anna said. "Go talk to Rebecca, and I'll be keeping you and Jake's family in my prayers. Oh, by the way, Matthew's brother Zachary is moving back to Sugarcreek in case you're interested," she added. "Just a thought…"

Hannah had heard Zachary Graber had grown up, and was no longer like his younger, wilder self. But it was too much for her to think about at that moment, so she didn't bother to address Anna's parting comment. "*Danke*, Anna. I'll be praying for you and your family, too." She gave her pregnant friend another awkward sort of hug before approaching Rebecca.

"Rebecca, *guder daag*. Can I help you with anything?" She broke into her friendliest smile, all while taking a closer look at the woman. A few years older than Jake, Rebecca was surely not as lovely as Lily. But the good news was Rebecca was a wonderful cook, and she was always kind to everyone's children, giving them extra goodies to take home after the worship meal. Most important, she was still single.

"Truth be told—" Rebecca leaned closer "—I'm not the most decisive person outside the kitchen. What do you think?" She pointed to two fabrics, one a washed-out blue and the other a blinding green.

"Well…" Neither color was a favorite of Hannah's. She tried not to frown. "It depends. What are you making?"

"I'm needing a new dress." Rebecca bit her lip.

"Why not come look at some new fabric we just got in. I'm thinking there's a color perfect for you."

Rebecca followed eagerly as Hannah led the way. Pulling out a bolt of plum-colored fabric, she thought it went well with Rebecca's blond hair and brown eyes. It was also a favorite color of Jake's.

"It's so pretty, Hannah." Rebecca gleamed. "I'll take it. It's perfect for my special occasion." Her voice sounded almost breathless.

"*Jah?* What occasion is that?" Hannah asked, making conversation as Rebecca followed her to the counter where Hannah began measuring out yards.

"It's for supper next week."

"That sounds nice."

"Honestly, Hannah, I'm hoping it's more than

nice." Rebecca's eyes seemed to shine with a mixture of excitement and apprehension. "Remember when you tried to match Karl Riehl and me last year? Well, I guess the timing wasn't right then. But now..." She clasped her hands as if in prayer. "He and I have been seeing each other a lot lately. He wants me to have supper with his parents."

Scissors in hand, Hannah paused, feeling her hope for Jake and his *kinner* slipping away. "Oh, I didn't know. That sounds serious."

"I hope it is. I pray it's *Gott*'s plan," Rebecca confided. "I've spent so many years alone, and Karl is such a *wunderbaar-gut* man."

At Rebecca's admission, what could Hannah do but reach out and pat her hand. "You and Karl would do well together, Rebecca," she said sincerely. "I'll be praying it's *Gott*'s plan for you both, too."

After Rebecca paid for her fabric and left, Hannah told herself that just as the Lord had brought Karl and Rebecca together, He'd surely be there for Jake and his children, as well. Still, it didn't keep her from sizing up the next few Amish women she waited on as possible matches for the Burkholder household.

Yet no one seemed to be a likely fit. It wasn't until later in the afternoon, when the rain had ceased and the skies were lightening, that the door opened once more and Hannah looked up, surprised.

Why, of course! Miriam Schrock, the school's elementary teacher. She was also single, and liked children, *jah*?

"Miriam," she exclaimed. "I'm so glad to see you!"

"You are?" Miriam shot her a puzzled look. The two of them had always known each other but had never been particularly close. Hannah tried to think why that was. At that moment, a reason escaped her.

"Yes, I am. It's been a long time, hasn't it? I'm happy to help you find whatever you might need. Come to think of it, I'd be mighty grateful if you could help me, too."

It had taken some convincing to get Miriam to say she'd come out to Jake's farm the next week for dessert. Oh, and just the smallest of fibs, too. Small because maybe if Hannah had thought to ask Sarah, perhaps the child really might say she was nervous about attending school the following year. Maybe if she'd asked, Sarah would say she wanted to meet her teacher in a comfortable setting like her own home.

A lie is a lie, no matter the size, Hannah. Her mother's voice rang in her ears. As she drove out to Jake's after work to tell him her news, she began praying again—this time for forgiveness.

* * *

At the muffled sound of horse hooves, Jake looked up from the pile of clean clothes he was folding and peered out the window. He didn't know what he'd done right to have so many pleasant visitors in one day, but he wasn't complaining. Especially not at the sight of Hannah's buggy not twenty-four hours after he'd last seen her.

Happy to take a break from laundry, he was eager to tell her his news. A gush of brisk air entered the house as he greeted her at the front door.

"Hallo." He smiled.

"I thought I'd stop and see if you have a minute."

"For you, more than one."

Slipping off her cloak, she gave him a crooked smile. He assumed she was wondering how he could be playful when he'd been in such a dark mood the night before.

"It's so quiet in here." She glanced around. "Where are the *kinner*?"

"Gone."

Her eyes widened. "Gone?"

"Jah, you wouldn't believe what happened."

Seeing her worried expression, he rushed to explain. "Don't worry. It's all good. At least, I think it will be."

She gave him a puzzled look.

"Seth Hochstetler's *mamm* came by for the

kinner a bit ago, and I think it's all going to work out."

"What do you mean?"

"Well, I was in town with the *kinner* today putting up flyers, hoping to stir up some handyman work, and I ran into Seth at Kauffman's Kitchen. At first I thought he was going to ask me about dating his sister—"

"Emma?" Hannah's eyes lit up. "I hadn't even thought of her."

"But instead, Seth told me he has an open position at the lumberyard, and he's really needing someone with experience. He'd like me to come back as soon as possible—tomorrow if I can."

"But what about the *kinner*?"

"When I was talking with him, I figured I could contact one of the nannies I've used before. Maybe for a short time, until I figure something out. Then Seth's *mamm* stopped by and said she could watch Sarah and the twins for the next month until she needs to care for her ill sister. She also said she'd help me find another nanny for them in the meantime." Hannah's pretty face brightened at his news, which erased the nagging doubts from his mind.

"Jake! That's great to hear!"

"And good timing, too. I wasn't quite sure how I was going to get through the winter financially," he admitted. "But *Gott* opened a door, and I need to take it on faith that something will work out long-term." He lifted his hands in surrender.

"And the *kinner* are with Mrs. Hochstetler now?"

He nodded. "*Jah*, they left just a little while ago. She wanted to spend some time with them so they could get acquainted."

"I'm sure it'll all be *gut*. Mrs. Hochstetler is a very nice woman, and your *kinner* are always delightful."

"Mostly." He chuckled before changing the subject. "Did you miss me already? Is that why you stopped by?"

"*Jah*. I mean *nee*. I mean—" Hannah stuttered as her cheeks bloomed with color.

"I'm only teasin', Hannah. You know, like you tease me."

Her lips eased into a more relaxed smile. "I actually stopped to let you know I have your first date set up."

"Already?" He almost audibly gulped.

"Well, not exactly a date, more like someone coming over for dessert next week."

"And who might that someone be?"

"Miriam Schrock is coming over to talk to Sarah about starting school next fall. And to visit with you, too."

"Miriam *Shock*?" He winced. "Really, Hannah?"

"Oh, that's right. People called her that for a reason, didn't they?" She cringed slightly. "Well, she's pretty as can be, Jake. And I'm sure she's changed by now. People do change, you know."

He didn't know if he quite agreed with that statement. From his experience he'd learned people only changed if they wanted to. Yet knowing Hannah was trying her best to help him and the children, he nodded assuredly. "All right, as long I don't have to make the dessert."

"Definitely not. I'll do the baking. You do want to make a good impression with her, don't you?"

He grinned. "I'll let you know when the time comes."

Just then, a noise sounded outside the window, capturing both of their attentions. Then he saw Mrs. Hochstetler's buggy pull into the yard.

Jake's good mood began sinking rapidly. "They haven't been gone that long."

"Maybe one of the *kinner* forgot something," Hannah offered. "Maybe one of them wanted gloves."

But by the time Mrs. Hochstetler got the children into the house and stood a good distance away from them, Jake knew the reason for their early return wasn't as simple as a pair of forgotten mittens.

"I'm sorry, Jake." Mrs. Hochstetler looked notably uneasy, wringing her hands. "I'm not going to be able to help you after all."

"I'm sorry, too, Mrs. Hochstetler." Sorely disappointed, he nodded understandingly. The three of them could be a handful at times. "Did you do something to upset Mrs. Hochstetler?" He confronted his *kinner*.

"Jake, it wasn't—" The older woman started to interrupt, but Jake held up his hand to stop her.

"If the children misbehaved, Mrs. Hochstetler, they need to apologize to you."

"But—"

He held out his hand to Seth's mother again.

"We didn't do anything to her, *Daed*." Sarah shook her head, looking sheepish.

"We only did it to us." Clara stepped in front of her big sister. "We scratched too much." She rubbed at the coat sleeve covering her arm.

"And I'm all hot." Eli began undoing his jacket.

Completely baffled, Jake finally did appeal to Seth's mother. "I'm afraid I don't understand."

"As soon as we got to Der Dutchman and the children took off their coats, they all began scratching. I started to notice red spots popping up on their necks and arms. Eli here is running a fever, too."

"Chicken pox?" Hannah stepped in front of him and felt Eli's forehead.

"I'm sure of it," Mrs. Hochstetler confirmed,

looking apologetic. "And since I've never had chicken pox and need to be in good health to take care of my sister in a few weeks, I can't take any chances. Again, I'm sorry, Jake."

"No need to apologize, Mrs. Hochstetler. I appreciate you trying."

"Do you want me to tell Seth you won't be able to start the job after all?" She bit her lip.

Out of the corner of his eye, he noticed Hannah getting the children out of their coats and shoes before sending them upstairs to get into their bed clothes. She was taking everything in stride while he was feeling like the world had just crashed in on him. Again. And suddenly, as the children traipsed off, she was standing alongside of him, seeming to take charge of his situation, as well.

"I may be able to help," she spoke up. "I had chicken pox when I was little. I have some vacation time coming to me. If I took care of the *kinner* until they weren't contagious anymore, then could you come just like you'd planned? For the last couple of weeks before going to your sister's?"

Mrs. Hochstetler glanced at him and then Hannah. "I think I could do that."

"If you'll give me a minute…" Hannah began slipping on her cloak. "I'm going to call Grace right now and see if I can begin taking vacation tomorrow. Then we'll all know if we have a workable plan."

Before he and Seth's *mamm* could even answer, Hannah was out the door, making a beeline to the phone shanty across the street. After ten minutes or so, he was concerned there was trouble with her boss. He was just about to run and tell her it wasn't worth all that when she came trudging into the house. Slowly. Her face suddenly pale, and minus the glow of determination that had been there before.

He was sure she had bad news for him. He was just about to tell her not to worry, when she spoke up.

"I talked with Grace and I, um… I can watch the *kinner*," she said quietly.

"It's all settled, then." Mrs. Hochstetler began to gather up her cloak. "Jake, I'll let Seth know you can be at the lumberyard tomorrow. And, Hannah, let me know when the children aren't contagious."

"Well, I—I don't know," Hannah stammered. "I'm not so sure about anything now."

"But I thought you just said—" Obviously confused, Mrs. Hochstetler was looking closely at Hannah.

"What I mean is, it seems I have more than a week to spare." Hannah's shoulders slumped more with each word. "As of today, I no longer have a job."

Chapter Three

"Try not to scratch, Clara."

Hannah attempted to dab at the rash on Clara's right arm with a cotton ball soaked in calamine lotion. But Clara wasn't making it easy—she was busy scratching at the bumps on her left arm.

"But it itches." Clara pouted, and Hannah couldn't blame her. Though her experience with chickenpox was ages ago, she still had a vague recollection of what the children were going through.

"I know it itches something awful. But it'll get better every day."

"Promise?"

"I promise," Hannah vowed, as she tucked a strand of hair behind Clara's ear. Hopefully every night would get better, too, for the children and for her. She sighed. She'd only been on chickenpox duty twelve hours and she was already exhausted.

Settling into a chair in the children's bedroom the evening before, she'd listened to them fidget most of the night. She'd also checked on their fevers every few hours, even placing a cool, damp cloth on Eli's forehead. Thankfully, the morning was starting out far better. Eli's raging fever had diminished to just below a hundred degrees, and the girls' fevers had subsided completely.

"I hope it's not too many more days," Sarah said, rubbing the sleep from her eyes.

"Sarah, try not to put your hands near your eyes." She strained to keep her voice calm.

Quickly, she finished dabbing Clara and moved to Sarah's side of the double bed.

"It's your turn, dear *maedel*. How about putting your arms straight out in front of you? And I'll get some lotion on you."

"On me, too?" Eli asked, sitting up in his twin bed.

"*Jah*, you, too." She smiled over at him while she finished covering Sarah's worst spots.

"Don't you have blue lotion for boys?" Eli asked the moment she sat down on the edge of his bed.

"Sorry, calamine only comes in pink." She began dotting the bumps on his neck.

"It's okay, Eli," his older sister chimed in. "Sometimes things just come in one color, but they're meant for everyone. Like the sky. *Gott* made it blue, but it's for girls, too."

"Sometimes it's pink," Clara chirped, which led to even more talk about all the various colors of the sky.

Hannah smiled at their conversation and was glad that between that distraction and the calamine, no one seemed to be scratching for the moment. Finishing up Eli, she let their chatter subside before mentioning food.

"Would anyone like breakfast in bed?"

"Did *Daed* get oatmeal last night at the store?" Eli asked.

"He did, but it's a kind of oatmeal that helps itching. You can take a bath in it later today."

"Fun!" Eli's eyes brightened immediately.

"But if it's oatmeal you want for breakfast, I spied some in the kitchen."

While Eli and Clara nodded, Sarah scrunched her nose. "My stomach doesn't feel so good. May I just have toast with jelly, Hannah?"

"Of course you may."

Placing the lotion and cotton balls on the dresser, she was just about to head to the kitchen when Jake appeared in the doorway.

"How is everyone this morning?" he asked.

It seemed he'd done everything he could to make a good first-day-on-the-job impression. His blond hair was neatly combed, his beard freshly trimmed, and his light gray shirt looked crisply ironed but wouldn't stay that way long while working with wood. She could detect lines around his eyes. That was understandable since it'd been after midnight before she finally convinced him to head to bed.

She wasn't about to mention anything he might find worrisome. Like how many times the children had woken up through the night. Or how many times her mind had kept her awake, while she cried over the fact that she no longer had a job to return to. It wasn't just the job. Her dream, everything she'd been working for, had disappeared in an instant. Jake had immediately offered his *dawdi haus* as a free place for her and her aunt to live. She'd accepted, but only after he agreed she would be the children's nanny for free. Even with that, she still felt orphaned all over again, her life out of her control.

She tamped down her disappointment for now and delivered good news instead.

"We're doing better," she said, injecting into her voice a note of optimism she didn't totally feel. "Eli's fever is under a hundred this morning, and the girls' fevers are gone."

"That's great." Jake's eyes instantly sparkled at her news and there was a lift to his voice. He was a caring father, for sure. "I thought I'd see if I could help with anything before heading out," he added.

"*Nee*. We're good. Ain't so, *kinner*?"

The three nodded, Sarah speaking for them. "Hannah is taking *gut* care of us, *Daed*."

"I'm sure she is." Jake glanced her way, giving her an appreciative smile.

"I was just about to head to the kitchen to make them some breakfast. Would you like anything?"

"I've eaten, but I can help you before I go," he offered, turning to the children first. "While I'm gone today, you *kinner* get some rest, and let Hannah get rest, too, you hear?"

"Jah, Daed."

Descending the stairs ahead of him, Hannah smiled at the sound of Jake's trio chiming in together. Once in the kitchen, she began pulling oatmeal and bread from the pantry.

"I can pour juice," Jake offered, coming into the kitchen. Reaching into the cabinet, he took out three glasses—which Hannah immediately took from his hands.

"Honestly, Jake, I can get this. You don't want to be late on your first day, do you?"

He glanced at the clock. She could tell he was anxious to leave, but he was stalling.

"It's okay." She nudged at his shoulder. "You need to be on your way now."

Still he didn't move, his eyes searching hers. "I feel badly about how things turned out, Hannah."

"I know you do, Jake. And as I've told you, losing my job wasn't anything to do with you. Or the children. Or even me. I should've seen it coming, honestly." She shrugged, thinking how naive she'd been. "And it's not even Grace's fault that she has to close the shop. The rent has nearly doubled. And with the opening of that fabric chain store…" She worked hard to put on a brave face. "And I'll tell you this, if you don't get out of here, you're not going to have a job, either."

His warm, grateful smile soothed her, kind of like how the calamine had seemed to help the children's discomfort. "All right. I'm going. Do you want me to pick up anything on my way home? Bananas or milk or—?"

"No, *danke*. The only thing you need to concentrate on is your job and having a *wunderbaar* first day. *Jah?*"

"But I could—"

She stopped him, pointing to the back door.

He held up his hands in submission, backing toward the exit. "Okay, I'm going."

She nodded.

But just as he was about to turn and grab his jacket and hat from the hook by the door, she called out to him. "Wait!"

"Jah?" He shifted around, looking eager. "Did you change your mind? What can I bring you?"

"It's not that." She shook her head. "It's your collar."

Stepping forward, she reached up and straightened his crooked collar. Being accustomed to the feel of fabric at her fingertips, she couldn't stop herself from running her hands over his shoulders, smoothing the cloth underneath his suspenders just so.

"There." She patted his broad shoulders. "Perfect."

"*Jah?* You really think so?" He stared into her eyes, a teasing grin curving his lips. The kind of smile that always used to make her cheeks flush, and unfortunately, still did.

"Jake Burkholder. Go. Now," she said as sternly as she could. After all, this new living arrangement wasn't apt to work if she was going to blush like the young schoolgirl she used to be.

Seth and the rest of the Hochstetler clan were on hand to welcome Jake, kindly making him feel like he was doing them a favor instead of the other way around. After a bit of catching up, Seth escorted him to the section of the lumberyard where he'd be working, introducing him to new team members, both Amish and *Englisch*. He also insisted Jake take some time to get reacquainted with his former coworkers, which he was glad to do.

No doubt it was especially good to see Tom McDaniel again. Although from different backgrounds, he and the *Englischer* had easily become good friends when they'd worked together over two years ago. Jake very much enjoyed the man's sense of humor, which was every bit as clever as any Amish proverb. Often as the two of them worked side by side, they had shared stories about their children, their marriages and their faith.

He figured Tom might've felt glad to see him, too. When Jake reached out to give Tom a handshake, Tom took Jake's hand and drew him in, patting Jake on the back. It felt like an instant resurrection of the friendship they'd shared. Tom had been the only person Jake had ever dared to confide in—about Lily's drug addiction. He'd seemed safe to tell, since Lily had pleaded with him not to let anyone in their Amish community know about her issue, promising she'd try harder. Promising she'd get better.

"Man, it's been a while." About the same age as Jake but a few inches shorter, Tom stepped back, giving Jake a once-over. "You're looking good, brother. Good and healthy."

"It's by *Gott*'s good grace. It sure isn't because of my cooking." Jake chuckled. "You're looking good yourself."

"Ashley takes full charge of that and is all about fat-free, gluten-free and whatever-else-free." Tom smiled, rolling his eyes. "From time to time, I have to sneak a burger and fries."

Jake laughed. "*Jah*, I hear you. We don't want to get too thin and scrawny, do we?"

"Exactly," Tom readily agreed with a grin. "Hey, I have an order that needs to be processed ASAP, but let's catch up later. You've been missed around here, buddy."

"I've missed the job, too." Jake nodded.

As Tom walked away and Jake got settled in at the planer, he realized the job wasn't the only thing he'd felt nostalgic about. He'd also missed the camaraderie. Even the scent of the various woods, and the opportunities to help customers, instantly seemed to renew his spirit, giving him an ear-to-ear smile that made the hours slip by quickly.

In fact, he was so engrossed in his work that it wasn't until he sensed someone come up directly beside him that he shut down the machine, pulled down his goggles and turned to see a familiar face.

"Rosie! Is that you?"

Standing with her arms crossed over her chest, Hochstetler's longtime personnel manager Rosie Thatcher didn't look much different since the last time he'd seen her. Maybe a little grayer and slightly chubbier, but the *Englisch* woman still radiated the perfect blend of professionalism and friendship.

"It's me, still alive and kicking," she clucked.

"It's *gut* to see you." He meant the words sincerely. Rosie had been like a dear aunt to him when he'd been going through shakier times.

"Well, if it's so good to see me, Jacob, why didn't you stop by my office before lunch? I need you to sign some papers and fill out forms."

"Oh, *jah*. Sorry about that." He frowned. "I can come sign things now. Unless you'd rather wait until tomorrow?"

"Never put off till tomorrow what you already don't want to do today. It probably won't get done."

He grinned at the truth of her statement. "Lead the way."

Expedient as ever, Rosie already had the required employee forms on her desk. It didn't take him long to fill in his information and sign them.

"And last, but not least, is the community fund pay form." Rosie handed him another sheet of paper. "Don't feel forced to contribute, Jacob. Or if you want to, you can do it later, you know, when you've been here a bit longer. I can imagine that things have been—"

He cut her off, taking the form from her hands. "I'm happy to sign up now."

Years ago, employees at Hochstetler's had started an emergency fund for lumberyard workers and their families as well as for others in their small community. Each pay period an employee could chip in whatever money they wished, and that amount would come directly out of their paycheck and be added to the fund.

When Lily had passed, some monies from that fund were given to him, helping him make the transition from working dad to stay-at-home dad easier. Knowing that people cared had made all the difference.

"How are your children?" Rosie asked as he handed her the completed form. "Are they doing all right?"

"Ah...they have chickenpox."

"Oh, goodness." Rosie shook her head. "Been there, done that. It's no fun, but it'll pass quickly."

"*Jah.* They'll be fine. I'm just used to being there with them. I'm kind of feeling guilty that I'm not." He felt funny admitting such a thing, but it was true.

"I'm sure you left them in capable hands," Rosie responded.

"I did. A good friend, Hannah Miller, is watching them."

"Hmm..." Rosie squinted. "Why does that name sound familiar to me?"

He found himself telling his surrogate aunt all about what had happened with the nannies, the children's illness, and how Hannah had offered to help and then lost her job. "I'm still not feeling right about it," he admitted, to which Rosie simply smiled at him.

"You know what this gray hair means, Jacob?" She pointed to the lighter hair edging the sides of her face. "This gray means I've lived long enough to know and believe that God's timing is far better than ours. If you're feeling that badly about it, pick up some flowers for Hannah on your way home tonight," she suggested.

"Flowers." He blinked. "We have mums in the garden."

"I'm sure you do. But it's not the same. Every woman likes a bouquet of flowers that's just for her."

He shrugged, tossing Rosie's suggestion around in his mind. "Hmm… Maybe you're right."

"Jacob, you've known me long enough to know I'm always right." Rosie's eyes glimmered as she chuckled.

All the way home, he debated with himself about stopping to buy flowers for Hannah.

But then a memory came back to him. Of a day long ago, and a field. And the elated look on Hannah's face when he picked a handful of wildflowers from that field and presented them to her. If witnessing that look was all that had happened to him that day, maybe he would've bought flowers just like Rosie said.

But that wasn't all that had taken place. When

he'd handed Hannah those flowers that day, an intense feeling had welled up inside him, making him want to give her every good thing there was on *Gott*'s blessed earth.

Yet, that wasn't meant to be. Not then, and certainly not now. He and Hannah were merely friends helping friends. Their situation was temporary, as it should be.

Even so, noticing the lights still on in Dee's Florist Shop, something inside him made him stop. Pulling into Dee's lot, he hitched his buggy to a post and headed for the store, thinking he'd buy a single rose. But right as he opened the shop door, the overhead chime jingled, and the sound brought him to his senses.

Closing the door swiftly, he walked away and guided his buggy straight home.

Chapter Four

"**W**hy, what pretty scenery, don't you think?"

Hannah was sitting in the back of the horse-drawn wagon, surrounded by boxes of her and her aunt's belongings. But close enough to hear *Aenti* Ruth chirp delightedly to Abram Mast, who was busy maneuvering the horses and their cargo up Jake's driveway. Hannah noticed how their former landlord, being a man of few words, merely scratched a graying sideburn then nodded before giving her aunt a shy smile.

"The *dawdi haus* looks *verra* nice, Hannah," her *aenti* continued, turning to her. "I haven't seen it in a while. I'm sure we'll like it here."

After living with her aunt for so many years, Hannah knew it was just like her mother's sister to make the best of things. It was a trait that reminded her so much of Hannah's own mother. Though she'd been a young girl when her mother passed, she could still remember times when the food spoiled, or the basement flooded, or a sibling was feverish and crying inconsolably, and how her mother would take it all in stride. *Mamm* would manage to find something to take away the hunger pangs, sweep up the floodwater without complaining, heal her siblings with hugs, and through it all, remind Hannah how important it was to count her blessings.

"*Jah*, it will be *gut*," Hannah agreed, trying to follow in her mother's and aunt's positive footsteps, and eager to convince herself, as well. Because while she'd been packing the night before and that morning, she couldn't stop feeling unsettled.

It wasn't so much that she'd miss living in town. Or that the rooms she'd rented for herself and her aunt in the Victorian house owned by Abram and his sister Susan had been all that spacious or irreplaceable.

But after so many years of being on her own, after working hard and being closer to achieving her dream using the talent *Gott* gave her, moving into Jake's property felt like a step backward. Now she had no idea what her future looked like anymore. And as much as she wanted to help Jake and his children—and knew he wanted to help her by giving her a place to live—she felt like she was depending on someone too much.

And didn't depending on someone usually lead to being disappointed somehow?

"Oh, Abram, look at all the colorful chrysanthemums and the beautiful, rolling hills," her aunt was exclaiming as if she'd never witnessed Sugarcreek's picturesque landscape before. "It's perfect!"

In spite of her mixed feelings, Hannah found her aunt's unbridled enthusiasm hard to resist, and began to look outside herself. Eyeing the land bordering Jake's property, she had to admit it did look mighty special.

The air might've been brisk, but the late-autumn afternoon sun sparkled on the outstretched fields and patchwork of hills in a way that could warm a person's soul—even hers.

"And there's our new landlord," *Aenti* Ruth said gaily, pointing toward the house. "Though you'll always be my first landlord in Sugarcreek, Abram." She smiled broadly at the man sitting beside her.

Jake's lean frame certainly wasn't hard to miss. Hammer in hand, he was bent over, and appeared to be putting the finishing touches on his latest project. It wasn't until he stood up that Hannah realized just what that project was. A wheelchair ramp that led up to the *dawdi haus* porch.

Hannah couldn't believe she'd been so wrapped up in herself the past few days that she hadn't ever considered how her aunt would get in and out of their new home. But clearly Jake had.

Right away, his thoughtfulness shifted her mood. He was such a kind, caring person. He truly deserved any happiness he could find and all that she'd promised to help him find.

Laying the hammer on the porch rail, Jake waved at them with a sly grin on his face. She easily recognized it from their youth as one that always meant he'd been up to something. This time, something good.

"It looks like you've been busy getting ready for my stay," *Aenti* Ruth called out to Jake as Abram brought the horses to a halt. As usual, her aunt was never one to be shy about her disability.

"And looking forward to it," he replied.

Feeling grateful that the two most important people in her life always got along no matter how much time passed, Hannah whispered, *"Danke,"* to Jake as he helped her down from the wagon.

He looked at her, puzzled. "I think I should be saying that to you, ain't so?"

Meanwhile, Abram had retrieved her aunt's wheelchair from the back before helping her settle into the chair. Hannah was surprised how he performed the task as if it was the most natural thing in the world. Any of the times she'd encountered her aunt and Abram together, either working on puzzles or people-watching from a porch bench, he seemed to be a quiet, awkward man.

"Jake, I don't know if you've met Abram Mast." She looked between the men. "And, Abram, this is Jake Burkholder."

"I think I've seen you at Hochstetler's Lumberyard," Jake said to the older man. "It's *gut* to see you again. Thanks for helping the ladies with their move. It gave me time to get the *haus* ready for them."

"Jah." Abram nodded.

Abram also hadn't had much to say when Hannah told him about losing her job and their need to move abruptly. He and his sister had been nothing but kind. Susan had even offered Abram's help to get them moved. That meant moving clothes, embroidery accessories and puzzles for her aunt, and Hannah's sewing machine, patterns and material. Lots and lots of material.

"Jake, I haven't seen your beautiful *kinner* in a while," her aunt spoke up, bridging the gap in conversation. "Hannah said they're feeling better."

"Jah, much better. They still have some scabs here and there, but Hannah nursed them back to health."

"Where are they?" Hannah asked. It seemed odd they hadn't come running outside to greet them on their arrival.

"You'll see."

Jake waved them toward the *dawdi haus*, and they followed him up the freshly built ramp to the top of the porch. Once there, he opened the front door.

"They've been waiting for you," he said as he extended his arm, inviting them inside.

As Hannah entered the house behind Abram and her aunt's wheelchair, she realized just how true that was. In an instant, every area of the small home became illuminated with an amber light coming from all directions.

She gasped and her aunt let out a surprised "Oh, my!"

Sarah stood in the sitting room and had turned on a light there. Clara held a lantern that shone throughout the connected kitchen. Meanwhile, Eli was calling to them from where a light glowed from the bedroom.

"I'm in here!" he shouted.

Right away, with the girls scampering ahead of her and her aunt wheeling behind, Hannah walked over to the bedroom door. None of them could help laughing. There was Eli, sprawled out on one of the twin beds.

"I got tired of standing and holding the lantern."

"And I don't blame you," Hannah told him.

Glancing inside the room, she saw that the

two headboards didn't match and neither did the quilts on the beds. Yet somehow, all the colors and designs complemented each other, giving the room a warm, homey feel. No wonder Eli had been tempted to get cozy while he was waiting.

As he jumped from the bed, Sarah tugged at Hannah's hand.

"Come see what else," she said, leading her into the bathroom. "We got you and *Aenti* Ruth washcloths and towels."

"And soap," Clara chimed in, holding on to the arm of *Aenti* Ruth's wheelchair. "It smells *gut*, too."

"And there's bread in the kitchen," Eli noted as they all ambled back into the kitchen and sitting room.

"It seems like you three have thought of everything," her aunt complimented the children, causing them to beam.

"*Daed* did lots," Sarah noted. "He brought the rug over since it was too heavy for us."

"I helped him," Eli added.

"No, you didn't." Clara dug in.

"*Daed,*" Eli whimpered a protest. "I helped, didn't I?"

Jake stepped forward, laying a hand on each of the twins' shoulders. "You three are all big helps," he said, his words instantly defusing the squabble.

With the house lit up, Hannah could see just how much work Jake had done to get the place in shape. Not only was every surface sparkling clean, but the braided rug from the spare bedroom of the main house did make the sitting area look inviting. The curtains were pulled open and looked free of any dust. The windows had been wiped down, too.

"You even thought to bring over my pillow."

Among the throw pillows lining the couch was her favorite decorated with golden sunflowers that Jake's mother had embroidered. From time to time, he'd tease her about how she'd always hug it when they'd sit and read their Bibles some evenings. "Well, it's not *my* pillow, but—"

"It's yours now." He smiled. "Oh, and if you're wondering why I didn't put the couch in the center of the room, it's because I thought your sewing machine would work best over there." He pointed to a bare area on the other side of the room. "I know you'll still be using the machine at my house sometimes. But if you're sewing here, that corner faces south, and you should get more light coming in the window there."

"Do you like it?" Sarah squeezed her hand again, questioning Hannah with her eyes.

Hannah tried to answer but couldn't. Suddenly she was too overwhelmed. They'd all worked so hard to brighten the once-deserted house and turn it into a comfortable home. It was all so sweet, so thoughtful. Instantly, her eyes became misty and a lump formed in her throat. How had she ever thought it would be a mistake to live here?

"She must not," Clara insisted. "She looks sad."

"*Nee*. That's how Hannah looks when she's happy," Jake answered, knowing her too well.

"Your *daed* is right. I am happy. Like *Aenti* Ruth said, you all have thought of everything. Every little thing. Thank you, Jake. And Sarah, Clara and Eli. Thank you so much."

The children's eyes lit up at the sound of their names. It touched her heart to see how much they had wanted to please her. She opened her arms, and the three of them stepped into her embrace for a group hug. Until Eli wriggled away.

"And, Abram—" she looked over to where the man still stood near the front door "—thank you, too. We couldn't have gotten here without you."

"Do you like the house, too, *Aenti* Ruth?" Clara turned to Hannah's aunt.

"*Jah*, I do," *Aenti* Ruth assured all of them. "It's *wunderbaar*!"

"Perfect!" Hannah said, realizing she was repeating her aunt's earlier remark.

Right then, it struck her that her aunt might have had reservations about the move, too. Living at Jake's, on the outskirts of town, her aunt would surely miss seeing her friends as much as she used to. And without sidewalks or nearby stores to visit, she wouldn't be getting out and about as much as she was accustomed to, either. But *Aenti* Ruth had never complained at all. Not one peep. Without hesitation, she'd said yes and trusted where life and *Gott* were taking her. It was something Hannah needed to remember.

"Hannah, that makes no sense," Jake said a bit brusquely, but it was truly out of the kindness of his heart. He and Abram had barely gotten the boxes from the wagon moved into the *dawdi haus* when the woman started making dinner plans.

"Why cook when we can have peanut butter and jelly sandwiches? Wouldn't you rather be unpacking and getting settled?" he asked, knowing she usually was one for getting a job done quickly.

But apparently not this time.

"I can do that anytime." She waved a hand. "Besides, I only want to make some chili. Nothing complicated," she countered. "All the ingredients are in your kitchen, and the meat is defrosted. I thought I'd have a chance to make it yesterday, but I never got to it with packing and all."

"So why not make it at my house, and we can eat there?"

She scrunched her entire face as if he'd said something distasteful. "Because I'd really like our first meal to be here with everyone who helped. Don't you think that would be nice?" She looked up at him with that hopeful glint in her hazel eyes that he'd never been able to resist.

"Whatever you'd like."

"Oh, *gut*." A smile burst across her face. "And you'll stay, too, right, Abram?"

Jake watched as Abram blinked, then glanced at Ruth for his answer.

"Of course he will," Ruth confirmed.

Hannah clapped her hands together, her eyes shining even more. "Let me see what cooking utensils we have before we head over to the house."

"We? I get to help you cook?" With Hannah being at his house often recently, he hadn't been in the kitchen much. But he certainly didn't mind helping out.

"Well, I, uh…" She seemed to be searching for a way to spare his feelings. It almost made him laugh.

"Hannah, trust me, it won't hurt my feelings if you don't want my help."

"*Nee*, but I do. You can help me carry over the ingredients from the house."

The sun was setting, nearly touching the ridge of hills as they made their way across his lawn.

It was a peaceful sight. Hannah must've been thinking the same thing.

"The *kinner* seem happy to have *Aenti* Ruth here," she said, sounding somewhat surprised. "They had her and Abram working puzzles with them."

"Why wouldn't they like her? She's a lot like you. Or I guess I should say, you're a lot like her. Very easy to talk to. *Verra* nice to be around."

She giggled at that. "Jake Burkholder, are you trying to sweet-talk me into baking a cake, too?"

He chuckled. "I think not. Remember, I was the one ready to settle for peanut butter and jelly sandwiches."

"Well, *gut*, because I'll be baking this week for Miriam's visit. You do remember she's coming, right?"

He couldn't help but groan.

"Was that a groan I heard?"

"*Nee.* Just cleared my throat."

She gave him a sideways glance and a wry grin, letting him know he wasn't fooling her. He gave her a half smile in return, while trying to push the thought of Miriam Schrock's dreaded visit from his mind.

Thankfully, that wasn't too difficult to do. As soon as they entered the house and walked into the kitchen, Hannah lifted an empty woven basket from on top of the refrigerator and handed it to him, putting him straight to work.

Without referring to a recipe, she pulled together a few cans of beans, canned tomatoes, spices and ground beef and placed them in the basket.

"Anything else?" he asked, the basket now several pounds heavier than before.

"Hmm." She tapped her forehead thoughtfully. "There was something I was just thinking of… oh!" She snapped her fingers. "I'm going to need a large container for the chili. A bowl with a lid would work real well."

She bent down and looked through the lower cabinets. A few random items tumbled out.

"Sorry," he apologized as he watched her attempt to stuff the items back onto the shelves. "The cabinets are overcrowded. I wasn't sure what to keep when we moved after Lily passed, and I didn't know what had been left behind here by my parents and brother. So I crammed it all in there," he admitted.

"It's a lot, for sure," she agreed. "If you want, when I have time, I'll go through the cabinets and pantry and organize things a little better."

"I'm sure my pots and pans and bowls and whatever else is in there would appreciate that. I would, too," he added, though he wasn't sure if she heard him with her head buried in the cabinet.

A minute later, she pulled out a large plastic bowl with a lid. "Here's exactly what I was looking for," she said, getting to her feet.

As she stood up, something rolled inside the bowl. In the silence of the kitchen, the sound caught their attention.

She looked up at him, her forehead pinched. "Wonder what that could be?"

He shrugged, acting as unconcerned as could be—while panic reared up inside him, a feeling he knew all too well. His heart raced. His chest tightened. And a familiar sick taste rose in the back of his throat.

Too many times he'd found Lily's pills hidden in strange places. During their marriage. After her death. Possibly now—in the bowl Hannah held?

He could never forget the time after Lily's surgery and shoulder recovery when Hannah had asked him if Lily seemed to be acting strange. A little more distant, Hannah had said. Not as much like herself.

Of course, he'd known exactly what she was saying, and he knew the pills were making Lily act that way. But he pretended it was of no concern.

At that time, he didn't know what to do. Whether

to be dishonest with Hannah, his and Lily's dearest friend, or disloyal to his wife, who had begged him to keep her addiction a secret while promising to get better.

Standing next to Hannah now, knowing how he'd lied to her, he almost wished there was a pill bottle hidden in the bowl. Everything inside him wanted to unburden himself. He wanted to be cleansed of the lies and secrets that lay between them.

While Hannah started to pull away the lid, his thoughts were scrambled as he tried to think of the right words to say. But nothing came. Still he needed to say something. Anything.

"Hannah, there's a chance it could be—"

Reaching into the bowl, she pulled out a small plastic horse. "Eli loves to hide things, doesn't he?" She shook her head, clearly amused.

"Uh, *jah*. He does at that." He returned her smile with a feeble grin, feeling sick at heart.

What would Hannah think if she knew what he was hiding? What would she think of him for not doing better by her best friend?

Chapter Five

Monday morning had come quickly. Gathering her things so she could get to Jake's before he left for work, Hannah felt torn about leaving her aunt.

"*Aenti* Ruth, you know you're welcome to come over to the house, don't you?"

"*Jah*. I may do that later."

"I can always run back and get you," Hannah offered as she slipped on her cloak.

"Not necessary. I can easily roll down the ramp outside this house and roll up the one Jake kindly built onto the main house." She wheeled over to the front door and pulled it open, inviting Hannah to be on her way. "I'm taking it slow this morning."

"Are you sure you're all right? Are you feeling okay?"

"Why wouldn't I be?"

"I don't know." Hannah shrugged. "It's a lot

of change. New people. New surroundings. New things to get used to."

"And who says new isn't a good thing?" Her aunt cocked her head. "Besides, Abram may stop by later. He said I forgot something at the house during the move."

This time it was Hannah's turn to cock her head, as she stood in the doorway. "I thought our rooms were bare when we left."

"Me, too." Her aunt blinked. "I have no idea what he's bringing."

Hannah couldn't imagine. "Well, if you change your mind about coming over…"

"Like I said, I'll stop by if I get too lonely. And I promise I won't get lost on the way over."

"Now you're making fun of me."

"Maybe just a little." Her aunt chuckled, shooing her out the door.

Though it was a short walk between the houses, Hannah pulled on her hood and dipped her head to ward off the chilly wind. Her chin was still tucked when she entered the house, causing her to bump into Jake, who was about to reach for his jacket from the rack by the door.

"Oh!" She could feel her cold cheeks instantly warm the moment she brushed up against him. "Sorry."

Steadying her on her feet, he readily apologized. "It's my fault. I've been rushing around, running late this morning."

"Me, too."

"I guess we should both slow down some, huh?" Still holding on to her arms, he smiled into her eyes.

Feeling her cheeks burn even more, she swiftly slipped out of his grasp.

"Not if you want to be on time," she warned.

All business, she handed him his jacket and hat, then hung her cloak in the empty space.

"Are the *kinner* still sleeping?" She straightened her *kapp*.

"I haven't heard them yet."

"I'll wake them in a bit. We have lots to do today with chores, playtime and baking dessert for our special guest tonight."

"Oh… Miriam." He groaned loudly as he slid into his jacket.

"Are you clearing your throat again?" she jested. "You seem to be doing that lots these past days."

"Have you noticed that, too?" His expression grew serious. "Maybe I'm getting sick. I could be contagious."

Hannah couldn't help but laugh. "You know that's not getting you out of your first date, doncha?"

"I had to try." He pulled his wool hat way

down on his head, conjuring up a most woeful look. "I'll see you after work. Unless I decide to run away from home."

"You wouldn't dare," she said.

"I know. I'd miss my *kinner*, and I'd miss teasing you." His eyes twinkled as he waved goodbye.

As she closed the door behind him, she couldn't stop thinking how he always left her smiling. She'd never felt that irresistible urge with Lucas Sutter, whom she'd courted briefly soon after she learned about Lily and Jake's engagement. And certainly, her time spent with good-looking but prideful John Lantz had turned out to be nothing to smile about. In fact, those attempts were just one—no, two—of the reasons she'd let matchmaking and her job fill her time.

But she and Jake had always communicated easily with one another. She could tell him whatever was in her heart. But that simply came from knowing each other so long, didn't it?

She was still musing over Jake's silliness when Eli shuffled into the kitchen. Per his usual morning greeting, he came close as if wanting a hug but was too shy to initiate one. She leaned over, embracing him the way she always did. "Good morning, sweet *buwe*. Did you have good sleep?"

He rubbed his clear blue eyes before speaking. "I had a dream."

"A good one?"

His golden-haired head bobbed. "I dreamed you lived in the house out there." He pointed toward the window. "And that a nice lady lives there, too."

"That wasn't a dream, Eli. It's true."

He backed up and looked at her guardedly. "Really?"

"Really."

The sparkle of relief and happiness that lit his eyes touched her deeply. When he reached out and hugged her around her waist, she was moved even more.

Just like with his twin, his four years on Earth had been wrought with endless change. True, she'd lost her *mamm* as a young girl, as well, but at least she'd been old enough to know her. The twins had only been two years old when their mother left their world. Ever since, a stream of nannies and neighbors had paraded in and out of their lives. But had there been anyone who could make them feel like they were safe and loved? No, there hadn't been anyone like that. And more than anyone, she knew how a child yearned for that.

That's why I need Your help to find the right mamm for these kinner, Gott.

She kissed the top of his head. "I hear your

sisters chattering upstairs. Think they're ready for breakfast?"

"*Jah!* Pancakes?" He searched her eyes, looking hopeful.

"Sure, if that's what you'd like." She started toward the refrigerator. "Why don't you go tell your sisters to get dressed while I start cooking."

"Do we need to make beds, too?" he hedged. "Or is it washday?"

Walking toward the refrigerator, she couldn't help but stop and grin at him. How he reminded her of Jake as a young boy, always trying to wiggle his way out of things. "No, sorry. It's not washday."

Even the way he groaned in response reminded her of his father.

After they ate breakfast and cleaned up the blueberries that somehow got smashed on the wooden floor, the morning went by quickly. At lunchtime when she mentioned a visitor was coming for dessert that evening, and she needed their help to make a pie, the children were thrilled. Sarah donned an apron that fell past her knees and the twins tied dish towels around their waists.

"Who's coming?" Sarah asked.

"A person we grew up with. Miriam Schrock."

Sarah's eyes immediately went wide. "I've heard of her from girls at worship who have her as a teacher."

Hannah started to ask Sarah exactly what she'd heard about Miriam, but Clara changed the subject.

"What kind of pie are we making?" the twin asked.

"A pumpkin custard pie," Hannah told them. "It's *Aenti* Ruth's recipe."

"Is *Aenti* Ruth going to help?" Eli asked.

"*Nee*, it looks like she has company."

All throughout the morning, each time Hannah glanced out the window, she'd spied Abram's buggy outside the *dawdi haus*. Her first instinct had been to run over and rescue her aunt. But as her aunt had reminded her earlier, she was capable of wheeling to the house on her own. Even so, *Aenti* Ruth had to be bored beyond belief, entertaining the nearly wordless man for so long.

In a way, Hannah blamed herself. She needed to set aside some time to make an introduction between her aunt and Joseph Beiler, Sew Easy's former repairman. He'd be a much better match for her lively aunt than Abram.

But even now, time was running short for baking, and she still had soup to make for dinner. While the twins played with flour that they'd spilled out over the tabletop, she and Sarah got to work, measuring ingredients at the counter.

"I remember my *mamm* made a cake once with chocolate icing that she called a pie," Sarah said wistfully as she poured brown sugar into the mixing bowl. "It had custard that was this high." She measured at least twelve inches into the air.

"I believe you." Hannah chuckled. "Your mom had a special talent for baking."

"But *Daed* said he couldn't find any of her recipes."

"Hmm, I honestly don't remember your *mamm* using recipes much. Or if she did, she turned them into big, fancy desserts like you're talking about." Thinking about baking with Lily brought a smile to Hannah's face. "I bet that dessert was yummy, wasn't it?"

"And messy, too." Sarah grinned.

Hannah laughed. "I don't think this pie is going to be that messy, but our kitchen is sure going to be." She leaned her head toward Sarah's younger siblings. Both were smacking their flour-covered hands together and laughing as the flour dust flew into the air.

"My *daed* says they rile each other up." Sarah shook her head, then rolled her eyes just like her *mamm* used to do.

Hannah had always noticed how the twins' features were a true combination of Jake and Lily. Yet when it came to Sarah, beyond her blue eyes, she didn't look like her mother or Jake, not with her dark curly hair and medium skin tone.

She didn't act like her mother, either. If it had

been Lily in Sarah's position, she would've snuck into the kitchen and tried to figure out the missing recipe on her own, using up all kinds of ingredients without anyone's permission. Lily truly had a hard time sitting still and being patient, and not diving in and going after what she wanted.

Even now, Sarah wasn't tossing around flour like her *schweschder* and *bruder* or even like her *mamm* would've. She'd already grabbed a wet cloth and was trying to clean up the mess. Knowing firsthand what it was like for Sarah to have to grow up fast, Hannah's heart ached for the second time that day.

After sliding the pie into the oven, she wiped her hands on a dish towel and turned to the girl. "Sarah, if you'd like, we can try to make that dessert of your *mamm*'s some day."

"We can?" Sarah's smile was as bright as the sun shining through the window. "Do you know the recipe?"

"No, but I'm thinking we can find something close and adapt it like your *mamm*'s. At least we can give it a mighty good try."

"That would be *gut*." Sarah grinned even more. *"Danke."*

The way Sarah's eyes glowed with such innocent appreciation made Hannah's eyes well up with tears. Partly because it felt *gut* to see the glimmer of pure happiness that shone on

Sarah's face when Hannah offered to bring her *mamm*'s memory to life. But also because as she glanced around the kitchen at the *kinner*, she was earnestly praying once again. Praying with her whole heart for *Gott* to be beside her and to guide her to do the very best she could by them—no matter what.

Other than the prospect of enjoying one of Hannah's *wunderbaar* desserts, Jake had been dreading Miriam Schrock's visit all day. And even more, when she walked in the door.

"Why, Miriam, don't you look nice," Hannah greeted her. "Doesn't she, Jake?"

Jake was silent as Hannah took their guest's cloak and turned to look at him. Usually he agreed with most anything she had to say. Even when he didn't, he rarely put up much of an argument, preferring to let Hannah have her way. But this time he had a hard time being prodded into saying something he wasn't feeling.

After all, Miriam Schrock looked the same as he remembered. Coal black hair. Blue eyes that might've been pretty but appeared too piercing and judgmental behind her glasses. If only her lips didn't look so tight as if she hardly ever smiled.

Mercifully, he didn't have to answer because Miriam spoke up. "I look the same way I always do when I'm finished with a long day of teaching." She peered over her glasses.

"I bet you could use a little something sweet, then," Hannah replied, thankfully, since he was still at a loss for words. "It can be a small reward for your hard work today. Isn't that right, Jake?" Hannah prodded him again.

"Dessert? *Jah.* I'm always in the mood for dessert."

Evidently, those hadn't been the right words to say. Both women eyed him, puzzled. Hannah even frowned, causing him to try again.

"What I meant to say is you deserve more than dessert. Teaching is no easy job. That's what my sister Esther says."

Miriam nodded. "*Jah*, if it were easy, everyone would be doing it."

Jake was ready to argue that *Gott* didn't call everyone to be teachers, but that everyone could teach children things. But he stopped himself, thinking better of it. "So, how about dessert?" He clapped his hands. "Hannah makes some *gut* ones. Doesn't she, *kinner*?"

His three children had been standing in formation like soldiers at the door when Miriam walked in. Sarah had made sure of that. He'd overheard her telling the twins that she'd heard Miss Schrock was hard, so they needed to act their best. He also knew she'd brushed their hair, replaced her and her sister's *kapps*, and had them all looking perfect.

Glancing down at his own rumpled work clothes, he realized he should've tried harder. Not so much for Miriam, but for the rest of his family, and for Hannah, since they were trying to be respectful of their guest.

"Why don't we all go into the kitchen and relax?" Hannah's soothing voice broke through the tension. "I made a pumpkin custard pie to celebrate your visit, Miriam. The children helped."

"You did?" Miriam glanced at his children, and for the first time he noticed a glimmer of something bordering kindness in her eyes.

All three nodded in unison.

"Eli and I mostly played in the flour and rolled the roller," Clara admitted.

Miriam furrowed a brow at his youngest daughter before looking around at all of them. "I appreciate the effort, and I hate to disappoint you all." She stood staunchly. "But pumpkin gives me indigestion."

Hannah's shoulders dipped. "I'm sorry to hear that. Well, I, um…" She paused, obviously thinking. "There are a few oatmeal raisin cookies in the cookie jar."

Jake chimed in. "*Nee*, I packed those in my lunch today."

"Of course you did," Miriam said coldly, like

she was already disappointed where he was concerned.

Hadn't he told Hannah this was the way things would go?

Still, for all of Hannah's effort, he needed to try to set things right.

"I'm really sorry about that," he replied. "But instead of dessert, why don't we all sit down and visit? It's been a long time since I've seen you, Miriam."

"Not really." She took a seat in the middle of the sofa. He and Hannah settled into chairs across from her while the children sat on the floor. "I saw you several weeks ago in town."

"Really? Why don't I remember that?"

"Because you didn't notice me. You were putting up flyers and standing not ten feet from me, but you didn't see me. But that's how things have always been with us. Isn't it?" She glared at him.

Hannah clapped her hands, moving the conversation elsewhere. "So, Miriam, this is Sarah. She'll be in your class next fall." She pointed to where Sarah was sitting. "And we—Jake— thought it best to make sure she knows all she needs to before school starts. Isn't that right, Jake?"

"Yes. My Sarah is a sweet and sensitive *maedel*, and smart, too. I think you'll really enjoy having her in your class."

"You do know your ABC's, right, Sarah?" Miriam quizzed.

"Of course she does."

"I was speaking to your daughter, Jake."

"Yes, Miss Schrock," Sarah replied quietly.

"And how to add numbers together?"

"We've worked on that some, but we'll be working on it more."

"Again, I was talking to your daughter." Miriam turned from him to look at Sarah again. "You'll want to know how to add, how to write the alphabet and your name. If you're a good father," she said, casting her critical eyes on him, "you will have already taught her those things."

"Are you saying I'm not a good father?" He could feel himself getting defensive. "Because those aren't the only things a father needs to teach his *kinner.*"

"I'm saying that being prepared would make her a better student than you ever were."

He could feel his face burn. Even if what she was saying were true about his school days, she needn't be saying it in front of his children. "You know what they say, Miriam. Teaching children to count is fine but teaching children what counts is better."

Hannah interrupted. "Would you all like some tea? Some soothing chamomile, maybe?"

Miriam shook her head. "I need to get home before it gets much darker."

"*Jah*, it's best you be on your way, then," Hannah said diplomatically, walking Miriam to the door.

As soon as Hannah closed the door behind Miriam, she leaned against it, letting out a long sigh. "All right…" She inhaled deeply. "Who wants dessert?"

"We do!" The *kinner* cried out and took off for the kitchen.

"Now do you remember why they call her *Shock*?" he whispered as they followed behind the children. "She has no filters. Just a stinging way about her."

"You're right." Hannah shook her head. "So right."

Once they were gathered around the table, Hannah cut each of them a healthy serving of pie. Before she could top the pieces with whipped cream, he pointed to the container, sitting on the table.

"May I?"

She smiled at him quizzically and nodded.

Reaching over to Eli's plate first, he sprayed an *E* on his son's wedge of piece. "What's that *E* for, *sohn*?"

"Eli." The boy grinned.

Leaning over to Clara's plate, he sprayed a big *C*.

"And what's that *C* stand for, *dochder*?"

"Clara."

"That's right."

"And you, *dochder*…" He swirled an *S* onto Sarah's slice.

"That's for me, *Daed*. Sarah."

"*Jah*, and *H* is for Hannah." He reached across the table and wrote an *H* on her pie. "Though I could've put an *M* for *matchmaker*," he said under his breath, giving her a conspiratorial wink.

"Not tonight, you couldn't." She grinned before getting up and grabbing another container of whipped cream from the refrigerator. She shook the can as she walked over to his side of the table.

"And here is a *J* for Jacob," she told the *kinner* as she sprayed away. "It could also be a *J* for *just right* because your father is just that. He is kind and considerate and loving and—"

"Fun!" he exclaimed.

With that, he sprang from his chair and began spraying more blobs of whipped cream on the children's pie and even on their noses, leaving them squealing. They were laughing even more when Hannah came at him, topping his nose with white cream, too.

As he chased Hannah around the table, and the two of them tried to spray each other, the children clapped and screeched. They were both laughing until finally, Hannah, nearly out of breath, called for a truce.

"You do know we have to clean up the mess after we eat, don't you?" he said as he and Hannah sat down, and they all dug into their pie. He didn't want his children thinking there wasn't a price to pay for silly behavior.

"But, *Daed*, we didn't make the mess." Sarah smirked. "You and Hannah did."

He laughed. "*Verra* smart, Sarah."

After the children were in bed, it didn't take long for him and Hannah to tidy up the kitchen.

"It was a fun night after all, wasn't it?" Hannah sighed.

"But I need to ask, you didn't really think Miriam would be a match for me, did you?"

"*Nee.*" She giggled. "I just thought I'd give you a practice round."

"It was more of a workout," he scoffed. "I can't believe she said that about me and my school days…even if it was true."

She laughed. "Well, let's just say if I was the one handing out report cards on the subject of Miriam and first dates—"

"I would've easily failed, huh?"

"And I'm glad you did. Goodness, she's a tough one. However—" Hannah held up a delicate finger.

"*Jah?* I'm all ears."

"On the subject of parenting, I'd give you an A plus. You're a great father, Jake."

He was quiet at first, beyond moved by her words. "That means a lot coming from you, Hannah. What you think is important to me."

"I think you're the best, Jake, and you deserve to find the best."

Their eyes locked and, for a brief moment, held. Then Hannah turned to take her cloak from the rack, the day ending in the same place it had begun.

From her tone he knew she'd been sincere. But as he stood on the porch and watched her walk over to the *dawdi haus*, his past mistakes and overwhelming guilt pulled at him as it always did. Leaving him feeling that he didn't deserve the best, not at all.

Especially not someone as perfect as Hannah.

Chapter Six

Hannah had experienced many life changes in the past couple of weeks. But standing in Grace's former store, where she used to happily serve customers, was still a change that wasn't easy to accept. Sighing, she ran her hand over some material that she'd spotted in a packing box that hadn't been sealed yet. "I always loved this cotton muslin. It's so soft and came in the prettiest prints."

"I know," Grace Newberry agreed. "Remember when it first came in? You couldn't wait to make a baby blanket and put it on display for everyone to feel."

Hannah smiled at the fond memory. Yet at the same time felt sad that memories were about the only thing she could smile about as she glanced around her previous workplace. What once was Sew Easy looked nothing like the shop she'd helped Grace run. All the shelves and cabinets had been disassembled. Gone, too, was the counter that she'd stood behind for so many years. It had been the place where she'd greeted customers, helped them decide on material and yardage, and where she'd been happy to listen to whatever was on their minds or in their hearts.

Now the shop that she thought would be hers was virtually empty. All except for the stacks of boxes filled with material and sewing accessories that Grace wanted to gift to her.

"Grace, you're giving me so much. I appreciate it, but couldn't you make money by selling the material to another store or online?"

"Hannah, honey, I don't want this fabric to go to anyone but you," Grace said sweetly but firmly, laying a hand on Hannah's shoulder. "I know you'll make such beautiful things with it. And now that you're living at Jake's, you'll have more storage space, right?"

"Well...*jah*." She wasn't quite sure where that would be. In the basement or barn, maybe?

"Giving the fabric to you will make me feel better about things. At least a little." Glancing around the place, Grace sighed heavily. "I just never imagined things would turn out this way." She shook her head. "My dream was to help you with your dream. You deserved it after all your years of dedication and hard work. I never counted on that chain store coming to town. And dealing with that huge rent hike."

Hannah almost felt worse for Grace than she did for herself. "I'm going to hold on to this material," she promised, "and someday we're going to open another shop together."

Grace reached out and squeezed Hannah's hand, giving her a wan smile. "That's so sweet of you. But I have to say, this whole situation has tuckered me out. I've decided to retire earlier than I intended. Harry and I are moving to Cleveland to be close to our grandkids."

Admittedly, when Hannah first walked into the storefront, it had gone through her mind that Grace looked paler and somewhat grayer than she'd ever seen her. She seemed worn out from all the disappointment and changes.

"Harry's been trying to talk you into that for years, hasn't he?"

"Ever since he retired himself." Grace gave another weak smile.

"I'm sure your son and his family will love having you close." Hannah meant every word. "But doncha think you'll need some material so you can make your grandchildren a few things?"

Grace snickered. "Trust me, I've packed up plenty of boxes for myself. I couldn't resist, even though Harry has made me promise that from now on sewing will be just one of my hobbies, not my main one. He's ready for us to play golf and bridge. Honestly, I wouldn't mind having time to bake. Garden. Read. Things I've been far too busy to do."

"That sounds *wunderbaar*. Can I move with you?"

Grace laughed. "I'd take you in a second if you weren't so busy yourself. Taking care of Jake's children and your aunt—I'd say you have your hands full."

"Now I just need to find time to sew."

"You'd better." Grace wagged a finger.

After loading as many boxes as they could into every corner of Hannah's buggy, Grace promised that Harry would deliver the rest to Jake's place later in the week.

Then it was time to say goodbye. Hannah's eyes misted immediately as Grace reached out to hug her. Like her, Grace didn't seem to want to let go.

"Hannah, I'm sorry," Grace whispered into Hannah's ear. "So, so sorry." She let go of a sob.

"Grace, please." Hannah's voice trembled as she patted the older woman's back. "There's nothing to be sorry about," she whispered in return. "You've always believed in me. You gave me hope for the future. Do you know what a comfort you've been in my life? You've been like a mother to me."

Saying that out loud surprised even her. But every word was true. In many ways, she couldn't remember feeling the same kind of closeness with Rachel Keim, even after living with the Keims for so many years.

"Now don't you go making me cry," Grace said, but as she loosened her hold and stepped back, rivulets of tears streaked her cheeks.

"But it's true. And I don't want you to be feeling bad." Hannah swiped at her own damp cheeks. "*Gott* will be there for both of us, I know He will. And we can always write to each other."

"And we will." Grace pulled a tissue from her coat pocket and wiped her nose. "Are you heading back to Jake's now?"

"In a bit." Hannah sniffled. "He suggested I put up flyers around town letting people know I'm available for seamstress jobs and to sew decorative home items."

"See, I told you that material would go to good use with you."

Grace beamed for the first time that morning. Still, Hannah's heart was reeling with emotion as she gave Grace a final hug and headed down the sidewalk with her satchel of tacks and flyers. She kept hearing her own words about *Gott* having a plan for her future swirling in her head. Some days she could believe that without question, with absolute faith. And then there were other days…she desperately longed to feel that trust completely.

As she tried to sort out that contradiction within herself, her thoughts were interrupted by a familiar-looking man walking toward her. Even though his head was somewhat hidden under his hat, she could see enough to be sure it was him.

She halted in her tracks.

"David?"

He stopped and looked up. "Hannah."

He may have been family, but their greeting was nothing like what she'd just experienced with her *Englisch* friend. Even though her hands were outstretched, David's remained buried deeply in his pockets.

True, they hadn't ever had the closest of relationships. She was never sure if that was because he was six years older than herself and Lily. Or because he hadn't been enthusiastic about her taking a spot at the Keim table. She'd also had a closeness with Noah that David never seemed to share. But then David always seemed to go up against his father while prodding his mother into taking his side. Generally, Rachel did.

Clasping her hands around her pouch again, she said, "I'm glad to see you're all right, David. I've been worried. You haven't answered my letters."

"I've been awful busy with my job and the *kinner* and *Mamm*."

"*Jah*, your *mamm*. How is she?"

"She's your *mamm*, too, Hannah."

Instantly, her face burned with embarrassment. "David, I'm sorry. I didn't mean that the way it sounded. She was—is—my *mamm*, and you do know I'd be happy to help you any way I can, don't you?"

He shrugged his shoulders. But deep down, he had to know she cared. Since he lived two hours away in Middlefield, she couldn't do much. But she did send letters regularly to check in with him, even though she never received a reply. And she'd also hired an *Englisch* driver twice in the past two years so she could visit Rachel, and David's family. Though his wife had been sweet both visits, David hadn't appeared all that happy to see her. As for Rachel, the stroke had left her unable to speak. Hannah had no idea if she comprehended anything Hannah said.

She tried again. "I hope everything is well with your *kinner* and your *fraa*, Mary."

His response was a curt nod, causing her stomach to tighten. She never understood why there was always such an undercurrent of unease between them that seemed to have gotten worse over the years.

"Gut," she replied. "In case you're wondering, your nieces and nephew are doing fine, too."

Numerous times she'd asked Jake if he'd heard from David. His answer was usually no, and he never appeared to want to elaborate on that.

At the mention of Jake and Lily's children, David's jaw tensed. "Do you talk to Jake often?"

"More now since I lost my job. *Aenti* Ruth and I are staying in his *dawdi haus*, which has been quite a blessing. I'm taking care of the children while he's at work."

"Are you and Jake…?" He paused, and she could tell what he was attempting to ask, which seemed somewhat strange.

"It's only a temporary situation, David. One that's handy for us both right now. Once I find a job, and he finds a permanent nanny, *Aenti* Ruth and I will be moving."

"Humph." He blinked and looked at the ground before raising his head. But it wasn't to look at her. Instead he glanced across the street at the Highland Realty sign. "I have an appointment with a new real estate agent. I don't want to be late."

"Jah, I understand." She knew it had probably been a burden for him with his parents' home still for sale after two years. "Please give *Mamm* a hug for me. And if there's anything I can—"

"There's nothing, Hannah. But I…" He peered

straight into her eyes, as if he wanted to say something more. But it was only for the briefest moment. Then it was gone. "*Mach's gut,* Hannah," he said. At the edge of the sidewalk, he looked both ways before jogging across the street.

Appointment or not, the way he appeared in such a hurry to be gone from her felt like he was trying to escape from something.

She'd gotten the same feeling from him around the time of Lily and Jake's wedding.

Only weeks before the ceremony, when she'd come back from Indiana to help Lily, David had already permanently moved to Middlefield after he and Mary quickly married. His decision to move away had disappointed, and even confused Noah and Rachel, who assumed their family would always stay close by.

Of course, David and Mary did come back for Lily's wedding, but they didn't stay long. Hannah remembered that even then, just like today, her *bruder* didn't have much to say to her.

The five-foot-tall double-door storage cabinet wasn't the most involved piece of furniture Jake had ever made. Even so, as he wiped a rag damp with Puritan Pine stain over its hardwood surface, he hoped Hannah would be pleased with it.

Ever since Grace Newberry had stopped by

the lumberyard, asking him to let Hannah know about the boxes of material she had waiting for her, he'd been moonlighting in the barn each night, building the cabinet. He doubted the cabinet would come close to holding the amount of material Grace had mentioned. But at least it would be storage space for some of Hannah's favorite fabrics.

He just needed to get it stained before Hannah got back from Grace's.

Thankfully, at Ruth's request, Abram had stopped by to help Jake move the cabinet into the *dawdi haus* once Hannah had set out for town. Ruth had also been keeping the children busy all morning, playing outside and feeding the barn kittens.

The children were in on the surprise and knew he needed to finish the staining before Hannah returned. So why they were knocking at the door, and testing his patience, he couldn't imagine.

"Come in," he shouted. "No need to knock."

With that, he expected the door to burst open and one of his children to scamper in, either in search of kitty treats or in need of a trip to the bathroom. Instead, the door squeaked slightly, and he barely heard footsteps wandering in.

Curious, he lifted his head from his work and was surprised—no, shocked—by what he saw.

Standing in the glow of sunlight streaming in the doorway was a woman. A very pretty woman.

"Oh! You're not supposed to be here." She sounded as taken aback as he was.

"I'm not?" He blinked.

"What I mean is, Hannah's *aenti* said I could come in to leave Hannah a note. She didn't mention you were inside."

Whoever she was, the woman looked as fresh as the morning. Strawberry blond hair peeking out from her *kapp*. Green eyes. Freckles dotting her nose.

"She'll be back shortly. Do you want to wait?" He inclined his head toward the couch. "Or I can get a pencil and paper for you."

"I only had a quick question for her. But… well…" She rubbed one gloved hand over the other. "I suppose I can ask you."

He quirked a brow. Laying the stain-covered rag aside, he picked up a clean towel to wipe his hands. "You can try me."

"What time are you and I meeting for supper at Der Dutchman on Monday? Hannah didn't say."

"Dinner? Monday?"

She chuckled nervously. "I'm thinking you don't know about the date Hannah set up for us."

He didn't know which was worse. Telling the truth that Hannah had never mentioned it. Or acting like he'd misplaced his brain. He went for the latter.

"That's right. You're... I'm sorry, sometimes I have a hard time with names. I think because I meet so many people at work."

"I'm Catherine. Catherine Zook."

"Right. Catherine. Pleased to meet you." Again, he didn't want to hurt her feelings. "I believe Hannah said six thirty. Does that sound all right with you? Should I pick you up?"

"*Nee*, I can get there myself. Except...it will be dark. And there might be a drop in temperature." She bit her lip. "Not that I'm that far from the restaurant, so I could walk. But then... if you're offering, that would be *gut*. Unless, of course, you're just saying that to be nice. Because then—"

He held up his hand. Surely, she was simply nervous to be talking so much? "I'll pick you up at six fifteen."

"All right." She grinned. "I live at 2020 Redbird Lane. The house is on the right side—well, that's only if you're turning off Bluebird. If you're coming from Songbird, then it's on the left. Oh, and there's a park bench on the corner of Blackbird that—"

Again, his hand went up. "I know exactly where Redbird Lane is."

"Okay, then I'll see you at six fifteen. On Monday. For dinner at six thirty. At Der Dutchman. That will be *gut*."

Catherine Zook repeated every bit of their plan as she backed out the door with a sweet smile on her face.

What a surprise! He'd never seen the woman before. Although in the past couple of years he hadn't been off his property much.

Maybe Hannah was onto something with her matchmaking after all, he thought, as he stood back eyeing each corner of the cabinet to see if he'd missed any areas. Though he had to wonder when she had time to think of him and to reach out to anyone on his behalf. She certainly was special, that was for sure. She was so good to her aunt. And great with his *kinner*. She was always putting someone else's needs first.

He picked up the staining rag and began smoothing over a few of the lighter spots, feeling glad he'd built the cabinet. In fact, he'd make as many as Hannah needed. It was only right that she have the chance to do the thing she loved, and the time to devote to it.

Right then and there, he made a promise to himself that he would help make that happen.

Hannah felt like she'd been gone forever, but as she guided her buggy up Jake's driveway, she was glad to see the *kinner* were happily playing.

It appeared they were running circles, literally, around her aunt, who was directing them in a game of Ring Around *Aenti* Ruthie. They were giggling as they all fell to the ground. Until they spotted her.

Her aunt said something that sent Eli dashing into the *dawdi haus*. Meanwhile, the girls stood still, watching as she unhitched the buggy and tied the horse to a post. It was so different than their usual greeting, leaving Hannah befuddled.

"Is everything all right?" she asked.

Before her aunt or the girls could answer, Eli came running out. "*Daed* needs you. Right now."

Immediately, her heart sank. What could've possibly gone wrong?

Hurrying toward the house, she could sense the foursome trailing behind her. When she opened the door, she braced herself for the worst, expecting to see a flooded floor, a burst pipe, or the remnants of a fire caused by embers escaping the fireplace. But there was no foul stench. No smoky odor hanging in the air.

Instead, there was only Jake's familiar soapy, balsam scent that never failed to catch her attention. That, along with the unexpected aroma of new wood and fresh stain coming from a cabinet that fit perfectly into her sewing corner.

She gasped, not believing her eyes. The aroma

of the wood and stain heightened as she stepped close, and so did her emotions.

"*Daed* made it for you." Sarah said what she'd already guessed. "It's for your material and thread and whatever else you use to sew."

"I can't believe you made this, Jake. It's so beautiful," she said, surprised by her unpredictable friend. "How? When? It must've taken you so long."

"*Nee.* I headed to the barn a few nights to work on it after I knew you'd gone to bed."

"A few nights?"

He shrugged. "Maybe more than a few."

She reached out to touch the smooth surface, but he caught her hand in his.

"The stain is just drying, so you'll want to wait a couple days to touch it or use it. But it has four shelves, and I can make more if you need them. I can even make another cabinet if you want."

"It's perfect, Jake. So perfect that I don't even know what to say. *Danke, danke, danke.*" She started to give him a hug, but Clara tugged on her sleeve.

"*Aenti* Ruth bribed us."

Hannah glanced at her aunt. "You did what?"

"It's true." *Aenti* Ruth rolled her eyes. "I bribed the *kinner.* I told them we'd get pizza tonight if they'd keep quiet about their *daed*'s surprise."

"Well, they certainly did." Hannah chuckled.

"It's pizza for dinner, for sure and certain. And I have a surprise of my own."

"Ice cream for dessert?" Eli asked.

"*Nee*, not exactly. It's more of a surprise for your *daed*." She turned to Jake.

"Do you mean the dinner you set up with Catherine?" His brows rose.

"Oh…" She swallowed hard. "How do you find out about that?"

"She stopped by asking about a time for Monday."

"I was going to tell you about her. I mean, ask you. But I was waiting for Miriam's visit to wear off." She gave him her most apologetic look. "I hope you're not mad."

"*Nee*, it's fine. I know you only want the best for me." He repeated the words she'd spoken to him. "And who knows? Maybe one day I'll be raving about your matchmaking skills like Simon Weaver."

"Ah, *jah*. Simon and Greta." She grinned, remembering. "But let me tell you, Jake, you have more skills than you know. Even besides creating beautiful furniture."

"I do?"

"Oh, *jah*." She could barely tell him fast enough. "You made those flyers for me, and I took them around town like you said. And when I was tacking one up in the *kaffe* shop, an *Englisch* woman who used to come into Sew Easy noticed. Right away, she hired me. She wants me to make several things for her children's rooms."

"Your first job?"

"*Jah*. What a blessing."

"Hannah, I'm so happy for you!" Jake exclaimed. Suddenly, he lifted her up with his strong, muscled arms and swung her around. Laughter sifted out of her and a few sentimental tears, too, as she found herself moved by knowing how much he wanted this for her.

"*Daed*, you're gonna make her dizzy," Sarah protested, watching them.

"Really?" Clara piped up. "I like when *Daed* does that to me."

"Me, too," Eli agreed. "But why are you twirling her, *Daed*?"

"Because Hannah has a job to do," Jake answered his son.

"A job is a *gut* thing?" Eli wrinkled his nose.

Hannah burst out laughing along with Jake and *Aenti* Ruth. As Jake set her back down to the floor, she noticed his arm still lingered around her waist.

"*Jah*, Eli, it's a *verra gut* thing," Jake said. "Wouldn't you agree, Hannah?"

As he looked down at her, she could see all the happiness he held for her in his sweet eyes.

"Jah, verra gut." But even as she said the words, her heart fluttered.

Was she talking about her new job? Or how she certainly wasn't minding the close warmth of him?

Chapter Seven

Hannah could only hope, for Jake's sake, that he would have an easier time communicating with Catherine Zook on this Monday evening than she was having with his *kinner*. She had lost count of how many times she'd tried to explain to the children about their father's absence at the supper table.

"But why isn't *Daed* eating with us?" Clara asked again, her forehead crinkling like the sweet potato fries on her plate. "Aren't roasted chicken and fries his favorites?"

"You're right," Hannah said from across the kitchen table. "He likes roasted chicken and fries very much. But your *daed* is going to have dinner with a pretty lady in town tonight."

"But you're pretty." Eli's perplexed expression mimicked his twin's. "And you're not all the way in town."

She had to smile at his logic and sweet compliment. "That's nice of you to say, Eli, but your *daed* and I are only friends."

Instantly, a snicker erupted. It came from her aunt, of course, who was sitting next to Clara. "*Verra, verra gut* friends," *Aenti* Ruth commented.

"And we've been that way for as long as we've known each other."

"That's what you've always said, over and over and over again…" Her aunt whispered the last part under her breath.

Hannah laid down her fork. "*Aenti* Ruth, is there something you'd like to say?"

"*Nee.*" Her aunt blinked with wide, innocent eyes. "I'm just agreeing with you, niece, and your claim that you two are just friends."

"And we are," Hannah assured her.

"But," Sarah spoke up, "you do things for us and live with us like a *mamm* does."

"No, I live in the *dawdi haus* with *Aenti* Ruth."

"It's still our house," Sarah was quick to point out.

"Well, *jah*, but…" All the questioning had squelched her appetite, and the children looked like they were only poking at the bits of food left on their plates. She got up from the table, hoping her movement could also move the conversation elsewhere. And it did—for the short time that she retrieved the ice cream from the freezer and scooped it into bowls for them. But as soon as the *kinner* began eating, the questions started again. This time directed at her instead of their *daed*.

"When are you going to court someone?" Sarah asked, scooping up a bite of vanilla ice cream.

The young girl sounded so much like her meddling aunt, who turned around from the sink where she was rinsing dishes. "That's a *gut* question, Sarah, and one I've also asked. I'm curious about that, too."

"I don't really have anyone in mind right now," Hannah stated. Which was an honest answer. One she assumed would immediately put the issue to rest.

"But when you do have someone in your mind," Sarah pushed, "will you still live here?"

"*Jah*. Will you?" Clara frowned, ice cream dripping from the corners of her mouth.

Eli looked up at her with questions in his eyes.

Seeing all three of their confused faces wrenched her heart, making her want to swoop them up into her arms. Glancing over at her aunt, she could see from her expression how the children's concerns tore at her heart, too.

"I promise you, *kinner*, I'm not planning on courting anyone for a long time. So you don't have to worry yourselves about that, okay? And you know what?" She attempted her second bribe of the evening. "The sooner you finish your desserts, the sooner we can have a practice session on the sewing machine, girls. And, Eli, you can be the man of the house and bring in firewood."

Each of them looked pleased with her answer as they focused on their desserts once more.

As she stepped over to the sink to help with the dishes, her aunt patted her hand. "They'll be *oll recht*," *Aenti* Ruth whispered, offering her most comforting smile.

"I know."

At least, that was what she kept telling herself. Right now, the *kinner* were confused and anxious about what was going on with their *daed* and her, as well. Under the circumstances, it was normal for them to worry that any security they felt could all go away in an instant. Yet she had to believe that when the time was right, and she did find a match for Jake, they would be happy, and their lives would feel more complete.

Although if that match happened to be Catherine Zook, she couldn't take much credit for it. It was Anna Graber who'd sent her cousin Hannah's way.

Hannah had to smile, remembering how Catherine had come all the way from town and knocked on the *dawdi haus* door one day while Jake was at work. She asked Hannah if she could 'try out for the position.' At first, Hannah assumed Catherine thought Hannah was still working at Sew Easy and was asking about a job at the shop. But *nee*. Catherine was asking if she could try out for the part of Jake's *fraa*, which Hannah thought was sweet. Even if the girl did chatter a bit much.

Of course, after the way Jake had looked when Miriam came to the house, Hannah wanted to make sure he presented himself in a better light for this first real date. She'd started by laying out his newest black pants along with his black suspenders and wool hat. She'd also ironed the shirt she liked best on him, his light blue one. The fabric was a soft denim and so was the shade of blue. Ever since she'd known him, any time he wore that color, she noted how it accentuated his sapphire eyes and blond hair.

Yet when he stepped into the kitchen before leaving for the date, her jaw dropped at the sight of him. He was wearing his black shoes, black pants—and a dull, washed-out beige shirt.

"I'm ready to go," he announced as he circled the table, kissing the children's heads. "You'll probably be asleep when I get home, *kinner*, so you be good for Hannah and *Aenti* Ruth this evening, you hear?"

She couldn't help but speak up. "You're not wearing it."

"Wearing what?"

"The blue shirt I ironed and laid out on your bed."

He shrugged indifferently. "Beige is fine."

"But it's too..." The word *boring* came to mind, but she searched for a kinder way to make her point. Laying aside the wet dishrag, she dried her hands with the end of her apron. "I don't know, Jake. That color looks like...well, like you didn't even try."

"Didn't try?" He held out his arms and looked down at his feet before pleading his case. "My shoes are freshly shined. I washed up, changed clothes and even trimmed my beard." He touched the golden hair that framed his strong jawline.

"Did you brush your teeth, *Daed*?" Eli asked, slurping ice cream from his spoon. "You always make us do that when we go somewhere."

"You're right, Eli. *Jah*, I brushed my teeth, too. So I'd say I'm ready. And I look fine, *jah*?"

Always the peacemaker, Sarah spoke up. "You look real nice, *Daed*."

"Danke, dochder." He nodded his thanks to Sarah then turned to Hannah for her final approval. "Miss Matchmaker?"

"Jah." She sighed, acquiescing. "You do."

What could she say? No matter the color of his shirt, Catherine Zook was sure to be attracted to

Jake's captivating presence, his arresting good looks and his caring smile.

Which was what she wanted, wasn't it?

Jake wasn't tired when he left for dinner, but he sure was by the time he headed home. Catherine was a nice woman and as pretty as they came, but the hours he'd spent with her had worn him out. Still, he hurried, hoping to get home before his children went to sleep. Yet by the time he got back to the house, he could hear their murmurings upstairs, sounding like they were already settling down. Not wishing to stir up things, he tiptoed up the steps and stood outside the bedroom door, listening in.

"Were you an older sister?" Sarah was asking Hannah.

"Or a younger one?" Clara wanted to know.

He wondered how Hannah would answer their questions. He was fairly certain she wouldn't share her experiences as an older sister with his children. At least not until they were old enough to be able to grasp and not be frightened by her horrifyingly sad story of loss.

Sneaking a peek into the room, he saw her thoughtfully eye his two girls as they lay side by side.

"Actually, for a while I wasn't anyone's sister," she said vaguely. "So I was *verra* thankful *Gott* blessed me with your mother's friendship. Your *mamm* was like a sister to me," she said. "And like sisters and brothers—" she looked over at Eli in his twin bed "—we watched out for each other just like the three of you always need to do."

Glancing back and forth between the children, she asked, "Now, who is ready to say prayers?"

"I am," Sarah declared.

"Me, too," Clara agreed.

"Jah," his son chimed in.

"Everyone ready?" She clasped her hands together, and he saw her wait patiently for his children to do the same before bowing her head.

"Dear *Gott,*" she said in a reverent tone, "weary now these children lay to rest, please close their eyes in slumber blessed. Lord, may Thy loving, watchful eye, guard the beds on which they lie. *Gott* bless Sarah. *Gott* bless Clara. And *Gott* bless Eli. Amen."

Their little voices joined in with breathy *aemens.* Even outside the door, he sensed a special kind of peaceful stillness settle over him.

He was still in a tranquil state when Hannah gave kisses all around and came out of the bedroom. Startled, she gasped at the sight of him.

Without a word, they crept downstairs.

"You're back so soon," she said as they ambled into the kitchen. "That was a quick dinner."

"It didn't feel fast." He frowned. "Catherine

kept talking and talking—and well, I can only listen so much. I guess it's not something I'm good at."

"Not true." Hannah readily defended him. "You listen, but you also like to take action. Look at how you've listened to me and knew I wanted to keep sewing. Then you made a beautiful cabinet for me. And if I'm being honest..." Her nose scrunched. "It did cross my mind that Catherine might be too chatty. But she also seemed so sweet and pretty."

He nodded. "*Jah*, I agree, but it's hard to get to know someone when you can't get a word in edgewise. You may hear all about them, but they don't have a chance to get to know you. Then you don't know how they'd react to you and if you two would be a fit."

Hannah's mouth suddenly went slack. "Jake, I've always known you're smart, but that's so insightful," she said, sounding astonished. "I'm impressed."

"Don't be," he said as a wave of guilt coursed through him and his years with Lily came to mind. "Unless...it would help my cause."

"Your cause?"

"Well, if you think I'm ahead of the curve," he hedged, "maybe this would be a good time for me to take a break from courting for a while."

"I wouldn't call what you've done courting exactly." She chuckled as she pulled her cloak from the wall rack.

He pulled his jacket down, as well. "How about I walk you home?"

"So you can talk me into backing off on finding you a match?" She quirked a brow.

"Of course not. It's dark and cold. I'm only trying to be polite."

She shook her head at him. "Hmm, why don't I believe that?"

As soon as they were out the door, he took the opportunity to change the subject.

"I wonder about you, Hannah."

"What about me?"

"Well, if you're a matchmaker, and a mighty good one from what I've heard, why not find a match for yourself?"

He noticed her stiffen at his question. "You sound like *Aenti* Ruth and the *kinner.* They were asking the same thing at dinner."

"Did you have an answer?"

"I'm happy being on my own," she said simply.

"Then why can't I be happy being on my own?"

That stopped her. "Jake, do I have to remind you about the night you were practically in tears saying you needed a woman in your life?"

"Me? In tears? Never," he countered. "And

how did we get back to talking about me? I was asking about you."

She shot him a wry smile. "You're the one who changed the subject."

"Oh, you're right. That was impolite and would not be a good move on a first date. Would it?" he teased and enjoyed hearing her laugh. "*Oll recht*, back to you. Why don't you want to find someone?"

As soon as they reached the porch of the *dawdi haus*, they strolled over to the railing. Hannah leaned against the wood rail, looking away from him into the darkness. "I'm fine the way things are. Finding love for others has helped me find my place in the world. It seems that's *Gott*'s plan for me right now," she said matter-of-factly. "Plus, I enjoy taking care of your children, and I'm getting more sewing jobs all the time. Things are *gut*."

"That still doesn't answer the question."

"I know." She sighed before turning to face him. "Promise you won't laugh?"

"Promise."

"The reason I haven't tried to have a serious relationship is because…" She paused. "I'm scared."

"You, Miss Matchmaker? Scared?" He chuckled, then stopped himself instantly when he saw her disappointed expression. "Hannah, I'm sorry. That was rude of me. You're serious, aren't you?"

"I am." She tilted her head. "But I understand it must sound silly. Here I am pushing you and others into love, and I'm so afraid of it. But I've lost so many people I've loved. My mother. Father. Sister. Brother. Friends. Lily. Even when I saw David the other day it reminded me that I'd lost the Keim family, too. Noah is gone. Rachel is lost to me. And David and I were never very close, and still aren't."

Her answer stunned him. He thought she was going to say her reluctance to find love was because she'd been hurt in a relationship. Because he'd always wondered what had gone wrong with that love of hers while she was away in Indiana. The one that David declared to him without hesitation would soon be her *mann*.

At that time, hearing about her relationship with someone else had certainly hurt him. Because right before she left to take care of her aunt, he'd hoped to have a chance to talk, to see where they stood with one another. But she seemed so upset about her sick aunt, it didn't seem like the right time to ask. And then, the right time never came.

He was working up the nerve to ask about her old beau, until he noticed tears trickling down her cheeks.

"Hannah, forgive me." He took her hand into his. "I shouldn't have pressed you."

"*Nee*, it's not that." She sniffed. "Here I am feeling sorry for myself, and you've lost people, too—most of all, your *fraa*, the mother of your children." She gazed into his eyes. "I'm so glad *Gott* has filled your heart with your *kinner*, Jake."

Her compassion touched him to his core. Hannah could never think of herself too long. She was always caring for others.

"*Jah, Gott* has done that, Hannah." He squeezed her hand, rubbing his thumb gently over hers. "I thank Him for my children every day, and pray He keeps them safe." He paused, feeling torn. He wanted to say so much more but wasn't sure if he should. Finally, he couldn't contain himself.

"But I also have you, Hannah. We have each other. With everything that's happened in our lives, here we are together. I'm grateful for that. *Verra* thankful for you." He didn't mean to sound so serious, but the words spilled from his heart.

Fortunately, she didn't draw back from his earnestness. Instead, she chose to lighten the moment.

"*Jah*, I suppose we'll always be friends as long as I promise not to talk too much," she teased.

He laughed. "I still remember the time in seventh grade when you weren't talking to me at all."

"What?" Her head jerked back. "I have no idea what you're talking about."

But he could tell, by the exaggerated way she narrowed her eyes and then avoided his gaze, that she very well recalled the week that her silent treatment had been so rough on him.

"Ah, yes, you do."

"I know." She offered an apologetic smile. "I think it was my strange way of getting your attention."

"And it worked. I tried hard to find a way to make you laugh or speak to me, until one day I finally figured it out."

"*Jah*, you fell to the ground right in front of me, and I had to ask if you were okay." She chuckled. "I didn't know you'd fallen on purpose till you looked up with a big grin on your face."

"I knew you well, Hannah. And I still do."

"You really do, Jake." Her voice was soft. "And I know you, too."

They were quick to look away from each other. Standing in hushed silence, they gazed into the moonlit sky.

"It's a nice night, isn't it?"

In his heart, he meant more than the countless stars and the crisp white of the moon.

"It…it is," she agreed, her voice suddenly quivering. He looked over to see her shivering.

"You're cold." His first instinct was to protect

her. To push up her collar to ward off the chill. But he stopped himself and dug his hands into his pockets. "You should go inside."

"I guess it is getting late." Her teeth chattered.

"It is. I'll see you tomorrow." He pulled open the screen door, urging her inside.

As he walked back home, he couldn't stop from musing about the evening. At the cozy restaurant with a plateful of delicious food sitting in front of him, he couldn't wait to get away from his date. Yet standing on a decades-old porch, when the hour was late and the air cold, he didn't want the time with Hannah to end.

He would've lingered with her until dawn.

Chapter Eight

"Is anything wrong?" Sitting next to Hannah in the buggy, Jake took his eyes off the road just long enough to glance at her.

"No." She shook her head. "Why?"

"You've been quiet the past few days."

"I have?" She pretended not to know what he was talking about. But it wasn't true, and on a Sunday, too, and on their way to worship.

Gott, forgive me! She lifted her eyes toward heaven.

Ever since their conversation on the porch Monday evening, she'd been going out of her way to avoid him. Because she couldn't stop thinking about everything that she'd really wanted to say. Namely, the real reason she had never tried to find love for herself and why she'd turned to matchmaking.

Because while she was good at pairing up the hearts of others, she certainly hadn't been good at judging love for herself. And where Jake was concerned, learning her love for him was all one-sided had been totally devastating, leaving her with a hollow heart and in a very dark place. And if that was how it felt to truly love someone and lose them, she wasn't sure if she could ever face that kind of misery again.

"I'm fine. Honest." She forced a smile. "I've just been *verra* busy."

"If I can help you with anything, let me know," he replied sweetly.

He was trying so hard to be there for her, she felt compelled to let down her barrier. "You mean like teaching you to sew so you can help with my projects?"

"Well…hmm. I think that's something I'll need to pray about this morning." He winked.

For the first time since Monday evening, she laughed. His teasing brought her back to the present, and she realized she needed to do everything she could to keep the past where it needed to be. Behind her.

Besides, she had so much to be thankful for.

Tiny flecks of snowflakes danced in the morning sunlight while staying clear of the roads.

She'd made it through another delightful week with Jake's children, who were chattering happily behind them.

By word of mouth, her client list was growing

steadily, and because of Grace's generosity she had plenty of fabric and materials to use.

Aenti Ruth was happy to have Abram take her to worship with the families she knew from town.

And as Jake worked his way up the Hershbergers' driveway, she realized how happy it made her to worship with the circle of families he knew.

Plus, peeking out the buggy, she noticed the new acquaintances she'd made in past weeks were now familiar faces. And she'd had the opportunity to congregate with long-lost friends, too.

"Jake! Can you stop the buggy, please?"

"I was just going to park up there." He pointed to a piece of level ground where buggies were already lined up.

"But I just saw Beth get out of a buggy."

"Yoder or Lapp?"

"Yoder," she said. Though they both very well knew Beth's married name had been King, they'd always known her as Yoder.

"She's back in town?"

"I'm sure it was her. Do you mind letting me out so I can say hello?"

Jake pulled on the reins, stopping the buggy, and she slipped out, running along the edge of the drive toward her friend. Beth didn't see her. Instead, she was bent down, picking up a glove she'd dropped.

"Beth Yoder," Hannah called out.

Beth stood up, a puzzled look on her face. She swiveled her head around until her eyes lit on Hannah. Right away, she broke into a huge grin. "Hannah, is it really you?"

"It's really me." Hannah rushed toward her friend.

Lily had introduced Hannah to Beth when they were young children in school, and the three girls had played together. As teenagers they became even closer, sharing walks and talks, and had gone to plenty of singings and other *youngie* events during their *rumspringa*.

"I can't believe it! It's so good to see you." Hannah threw her arms around Beth.

"It's *wunderbaar* to see you, too. I've been meaning to come by and visit, but they've been keeping me busy at Kauffman's."

"Kauffman's Kitchen? Does that mean—?" Hannah hoped she was hearing right.

"*Jah*, that's another reason I wanted to stop by. I wanted to let you know I've officially moved back to Sugarcreek. I'm staying with *Mamm* and *Daed*."

"Beth, that's wonderful. I'm so happy for you, for me, for everyone."

Beth's mother, Lovina Yoder, had come into Sew Easy every so often. When she did, she'd give Hannah updates on Beth's life. About a year before Lily and Jake had married, Beth had met a man named Aaron King when she was visiting her cousin in Pinecraft, Florida. They married quickly and happily stayed that way for many years. Until, their life together ended abruptly.

It had been an extremely sad day when Lovina visited the shop to let Hannah know Beth's husband had passed. He'd died from an unsuspected congenital heart condition. Husbandless, childless, Beth stayed with her cousin in Florida for a few years. Hannah could only suppose it had been easier on Beth to mourn in a place where she felt closest to her husband.

It was still so hard to believe someone so young was already widowed.

Just…like… Jake.

Her heart leaped. And an idea suddenly came to mind.

She knew Jake wanted to take a break from matchmaking. But with Beth it would be different. Beth wasn't someone new he'd have to get to know. He already knew her.

Then maybe, just maybe—she shuddered slightly at the thought—if Jake was brave enough to get settled into a new life and love, could she? Could she finally take a step, make a real effort and be courageous enough to find a home for her heart, as well?

"Beth, I'm sure we'll have time to talk after

worship, but just in case, would you like to have dinner with me and Jake?"

Her friend's eyes lit up. "I think it would be *wunderbaar*. Let me know what I can bring. Dessert, a main dish, or something."

Hannah giggled at her friend's eagerness. "How about just yourself? I know Jake would love to see you."

"And Caleb Bontrager is in town this week. He's here at worship, in fact. What would you think if I invite him along?" Beth suggested. "The four of us together would be like old times."

Hannah knew the Bontrager and Yoder families had been close-knit friends for years. With Caleb, too, at dinner, Jake would be oblivious to her matching him up with Beth.

"I know Jake would love to see you both."

"I did hear you're helping Jake with his children and living with your aunt in his *dawdi haus*."

Nothing stayed a secret for long in Sugarcreek. "*Jah*, that's true."

"How *is* Jake?" Beth asked, as she glanced across the drive, eyeing him and the children exiting the buggy. "I'm sure he loves having you close by, Hannah. You two were so—"

Hannah held up both hands in protest. "We're friends who are helping each other right now. That's all."

"I think about him often." Everything about Beth's expression turned instantly empathetic, and Hannah detected fine lines around Beth's bluish-green eyes. "And about Lily, too. She was so full of life. Just like my Aaron." She shook her head and sighed. "Oh, goodness, we had some fun times with Lily, didn't we? Do you remember when she got a hold of that pack of cigarettes during our *rumspringa*? She talked the cashier at the gas station into giving them to us even though we were underage and didn't have enough money between us to buy them."

That was Lily. She could charm a bird out of the trees. "How could I forget? I've never been so sick."

"Oh, me, either." Beth chuckled. "But I don't think Lily even coughed once. She seemed like a natural. A part of me always thought she was more like some sophisticated city girl." She paused, looking away for a moment as if conjuring up the scene again.

But Hannah didn't have to work at all to recall that summer night. It wasn't so much for their smoking that she remembered that day as for the way Lily had seemed to be somewhere else entirely—even though she was sitting on the ground right next to Hannah. Leaning forward with her elbows on her knees, Lily had taken long, even drags on her cigarette, exhaling perfect swirls of white smoke into the night air. While staring at the night sky, she'd spoken about *Englischers* and *Englisch* boys, as if longing for something more. That had always stuck in Hannah's mind because it was hard to understand. She'd thought Lily already had a perfect, blessed life.

"It's all so hard to believe, isn't it?" Beth said wistfully.

"*Jah*, it is. But I'm *verra* glad you're back, Beth." Hannah sighed, thinking what a blessing it was to have such a dear friend in her life again. And how she should never question what *Gott* had around the corner for her.

"It took some time." Beth smiled. "But I'm glad to be back, too."

"Well, it looks like everyone is starting to assemble." Hannah glanced toward the barn. "I should go help with the *kinner.*"

"And I should catch up with my parents," Beth replied. "But I'll see you inside, and after worship, let's ask Jake and Caleb which evening will be best for dinner."

"That sounds *gut.*" Hannah nodded.

Midweek, eyeing his reflection in the bedroom mirror, Jake buttoned the top button of his neatly pressed blue shirt. Then unbuttoned it. And buttoned it again, telling himself he was being ridiculous. But he couldn't seem to help it. This dinner with Beth and Caleb seemed mighty important to Hannah.

By the time he'd arrived home from work, Hannah had everything under control. The scent of a freshly baked apple pie, along with the mouthwatering aroma of a roast baking in the oven, had made his stomach growl the moment he'd walked through the back door. The kitchen was all tidied up, and the *kinner* had already been fed and were settled in the extra bedroom upstairs, where Sarah was supervising the twins, coloring and playing games.

Hannah had certainly done everything imaginable to make the evening special for him and their guests. The least he could do was look his most presentable. So—as for his shirt—the top button would stay closed, he decided, giving himself a satisfied nod in the mirror before heading downstairs.

"Don't you look nice," Hannah complimented him the moment he strolled into the kitchen.

He noticed how her hazel eyes seemed to shine with appreciation, making him glad he'd put some extra thought into dressing his best for the occasion. He also couldn't help but notice how graceful and pleased she always appeared to be. As if she felt blessed doing even the simplest of things, like making her way around the table with a pitcher in her hands, filling glasses with water.

"You look mighty nice, too," he said sincerely. "Is that new?" He nodded toward her dress. "I don't think I've seen that violet color on you before."

"You're right, you haven't." She gave him a surprised look. "I came across this fabric when I was making something for the Gentry family."

"It looks *verra gut* on you." He smiled.

"You know, if I'm remembering right," she said, barely glancing his way, "I'm thinking blue is Beth's favorite color."

"Ain't so? I wonder if it's Caleb's favorite, too?" he teased, pleased at the sound of her giggle.

"We'll have to ask him," she joked back.

He veered them away from their silliness. "Can I help you with anything?"

"Nee." Hannah set the pitcher on the counter and smoothed out her apron. "I think everything's set."

"It sure looks like it," he said, glancing around the perfectly cozy, clean kitchen. "And it smells way too *gut* in here." His mouth watered. "I say if our company isn't on time, we dig in and leave them the leftovers," he added, making her chuckle again.

"Jah, well, hopefully they will be on time.

Because I'm just waiting for the rolls to finish baking."

The timer went off at the exact moment a knock came at the front door, leaving her to fetch the rolls and him the door. Then Hannah joined him and their guests quickly, and after hugs, handshakes and hellos, the visitors hung up their coats and she swept them all into the kitchen. Jake didn't know how she did it, but she seated them around the table, had them bow their heads for grace, filled their plates and had the conversation going instantly. It was as if she entertained all the time, causing him to marvel at her once more.

"*Danke* for going to all this trouble." Beth looked across the table at him and Hannah. "It's mighty nice to share supper like this."

"It was all Hannah," Jake confessed.

Hannah shrugged. "It's worth it, having the chance to see you both. After all these years, you two don't look a bit different. You still look wise behind those glasses of yours, Caleb, and you still have plenty of wavy brown hair that girls love."

"That's news to me." Caleb chuckled.

"And, Beth, you're still as pretty as a picture, don't you think, Jake?" Hannah turned to him.

Although Beth had blondish brown hair and blue eyes with hints of green, and features far different from Hannah's, both of their looks could certainly catch a man's attention.

"*Gott* has bestowed much beauty on both of you. Isn't that right, Caleb?" Jake asked his friend.

Caleb didn't have a beard to cover the flush of red that ran across his face. "I'd say so." To which the girls giggled.

"Caleb, I know Beth is back to stay, but will you be in Sugarcreek much longer?" Hannah asked.

"Only until tomorrow," Caleb replied. "Then I'll have to head back to Lancaster."

Beth let out a sigh. "This is like a reunion dinner and goodbye dinner all in one."

"I hate to hear that." Hannah held up the bread plate to see if anyone wanted extra. Jake took a piece. "Jake said you're running a butcher shop up there. You've been in the meat business for a long time, *jah*?"

Even when they were younger, Jake thought Caleb had a bold business sense but was shy around girls. Yet, surprisingly, as soon as Caleb was old enough, he'd set his sights on a girl named Fannie. When her family moved to Pennsylvania, he moved, as well, planning their future together while learning the butcher trade there. Only problem was, Caleb hadn't had the courage to ask Fannie how she felt about him. As it turned out, she hadn't felt the same, but since he'd excelled at his job, he stayed there anyway.

"Since I left in my late teens." Caleb nodded.

"Well, maybe someday you'll come back here. Like Beth has," Hannah chirped.

Beth coughed on a piece of carrot, and she and Caleb both shot a glance at him. Jake couldn't blame them. It was like Hannah had read Caleb's mind.

After worship the Sunday before, Caleb had revealed everything to Jake, telling him how he and Beth had been writing to each other ever since Aaron's passing. At first their correspondence was courteous and innocent like their longtime friendship had always been. But over time, their letters became more personal, then romantic.

Because of that, when the company Caleb was working for had started talking about opening another butcher shop, he offered to set it up in Sugarcreek. That was why he was in town—to look for a storefront.

Beth knew about his plans to open a shop in town, but Caleb was keeping it a secret from his parents, wanting to surprise them. He'd only told Jake, hoping to hire him to build-out whatever shop space he found. What Beth didn't know and what Caleb had shared with Jake confidentially was that when Caleb finally relocated, he was going to ask Beth to marry him.

Fortunately, Hannah didn't appear to notice their darting looks around the table. "Beth, I told you that Jake is working at Hochstetler's Lumberyard, didn't I?" Hannah asked. "So he's not too far from Kauffman's."

"You did tell me." Beth nodded.

"Oh, and he's so good at his job, too." Hannah leaned in. "They're talking about promoting him already."

"Is that so?" Beth smiled at him.

"Congratulations," Caleb said before lifting a forkful of potatoes to his mouth.

"It's only because I've worked in that same position before," Jake explained, as he carved the last of his meat into two bite-size pieces. "It happens to be good timing since another fellow is moving away."

"I'm sure that's not the only reason," Hannah broke in, appearing intent on speaking on his behalf, again. Especially to Beth. "It's also because they know he's good at whatever job he does, and he's mighty *gut* with people." She winked at her girlfriend. "Remember how Jake used to get the younger boys to help him with his chores, telling them they'd grow up to be big and strong like him?"

Beth covered her mouth with her napkin and laughed. "Do I ever!"

"I wish that had worked for me," Caleb jested.

"You all are embarrassing me." Jake chuckled, shaking his head.

But being embarrassed was the last thing on his mind as he suddenly realized that Hannah was up to her matchmaking antics again. Even though she'd agreed on him taking a break.

Otherwise, would she have ever mentioned blue being Beth's favorite color, Kauffman's being so close to Hochstetler's, all about his promotion, and even be talking about his physique?

Oh, but he could be just as sneaky and use her ploys to his advantage.

As Beth and Caleb pushed back their plates, complimenting Hannah on the meal, he did the same.

"And wait till you taste Hannah's apple pie," he remarked. "She makes the tastiest pies in the county, maybe even all of Ohio."

He was sure his praise would make her blush, but instead he noticed Hannah wasn't even listening. He followed her eyes, looking toward the staircase. Sarah was walking toward them, clutching her hands together tightly, her eyes wide with fright.

"*Dochder*, are you all right?"

Creeping up to the table, she stood on tiptoes beside his chair, bending close to whisper in his ear.

"That's not polite, Sarah." He shook a warning finger. "If there's something you need to say, let's—"

He started to scoot back his chair and guide her into the other room to talk privately. Before he could, tears filled her eyes.

"It's Eli, *Daed*. I tried to watch him best I could. I did!" She wrung her little hands. "But he—" She choked on a sob.

He leaped up, grabbing a hold of her shoulders. "He what, Sarah?"

"It's pills," she cried, taking a plastic bag from her pocket. "He found more pills."

Chapter Nine

Panic jolted through Hannah like a bolt of lightning.

The pills Jake snatched from Sarah's hand were the same color and shape as the ones she'd seen by Lily's bedside years earlier. No wonder that he raced up the stairs, two steps at a time.

Meanwhile, Sarah was standing, crying her little heart out. Beth and Caleb were both staring at her, wide-eyed and speechless. Exactly how she felt.

Tossing her napkin on the table, she jumped out of her chair and rushed to Sarah. Kneeling, she hugged the weeping *kind* tightly in her arms.

"It's going to be okay. You didn't do anything wrong," she said, as soothingly as she could manage, though her jaw felt clenched with fright. Looking into Sarah's fear-filled eyes, she tried to wipe away the girl's tears with a trembling hand. "Your *daed* will take care of everything. You'll see."

As she said the words out loud, those same words became a silent prayer, begging *Gott* with every part of her being for His help and presence where Eli was concerned. "But you need to go sit with Beth, child."

Thankfully, Beth was already at their sides. Still, Sarah clutched onto Hannah's waist, not about to let her go. "I want to be with you, Hannah. Please."

Hannah reached down, gently removing Sarah's hands and taking them into her own. "Sarah, it's important I help your *daed* right now."

With that said, Beth touched Sarah's shoulder, rubbing it ever so softly. "Let me get you something to drink, sweet *maedel*. Maybe some cocoa on this chilly night? I'm sure Hannah has some in the pantry. It was always her favorite."

While Beth led Sarah to a seat at the table, Hannah dashed up the stairs, rushing to a corner of the small room, where Clara stood bawling.

"*Daed*'s scaring me. He's scaring me," she cried, and Hannah knew why.

Standing in the middle of the room, Jake was roaring like a wild animal on a rampage as he hovered over a wailing Eli. Obviously, his ear-shattering rant was due to his own fear and desperation. But there was no way to explain that to a four-year-old.

Leaning over, she gently lifted the young girl's chin, looking into her eyes. "Guess what? My friend Beth is downstairs making hot chocolate for Sarah. Can you stop crying and go get some?"

Clara quieted some at her kindly touch. The mention of hot chocolate helped, too.

"With marshmallows?" Clara sniffled.

"They're in the pantry," Hannah assured her.

With Clara going downstairs and both girls in Beth's care, Hannah felt like she could finally go to Jake's aid.

Yet she was at a loss, not knowing what to do as he stood, shaking the bag of pills, frantically.

"Eli, tell me! Tell me now!" Jake demanded. "How many did you take?"

Clearly, the children weren't used to their father behaving like a monster gone mad. Just like his sister, Eli was wide-eyed and terrified. As he gasped and sobbed uncontrollably, Hannah didn't think he could speak even if he wanted to.

Finally, Jake seemed to realize the same thing. Attempting to calm himself, he tossed the pill bag onto the dresser, rubbing his hand over his face. Then he took in a deep breath and let it out slowly.

"All right, *sohn*. Let's both settle down," he said, his voice low and suppressed as he got on his knees. "Just say the number, Eli. How many pills did you swallow?"

Once more Eli shook his head, and Jake's panic suddenly flared again like a lit match thrown on gasoline.

"Answer me." Jake grabbed his son by his arms, shaking him. "You've got to answer me," he shouted.

No doubt Jake's own fear was scaring Eli into his mute state. Knowing time was of the essence in this situation, she realized they needed another approach.

Kneeling alongside Jake, she tried to keep her voice from quaking as she spoke as calmly to the child as she could manage. "Eli, we know you're a smart boy. Why, you can count way past ten." She reached out and pushed back a lock of fallen hair from his forehead. "Can you tell us how many pills you took? Was it one? Two? Three?"

Again, Eli shook his head through his tears.

"Oh, dear *Gott* in heaven, help us!" Jake yelled. "Are you saying more than three? We're leaving for the hospital right now. Hannah, get his coat."

"Nee!" Eli screamed. *"Nee!"*

Working to wrench his arms from his father's grasp, Eli cried even harder. Managing to free one hand, he raised it for them both to see. With his thumb and index finger, he made a zero.

"None? You didn't eat any?" Jake let out an

audible breath. "You're sure? *Gott* wants you to be truthful. Please don't lie, *sohn*."

"*Jah*, Eli. Sometimes we get fooled," she interjected. "You may have thought the pills were candy. But pills can be dangerous if they're not medicine you need to be taking. I know your *daed's* not going to be mad if you swallowed some, Eli." She tried to reassure him. "Your *daed* loves you no matter what."

"I…didn't…swallow any." Eli's little chest heaved. And heaved some more, as he desperately tried to catch his breath.

"You're sure?" Jake tilted his head, his voice stern but quieter now.

Eli nodded, swiping at his cheeks.

Instantly, Hannah's eyes filled with tears of relief. Even more tears streamed down her cheeks as she watched Jake take his son into his arms.

"*Danke*, dear *Gott*. *Danke* for keeping my boy safe." His voice quaked as he rocked Eli back and forth.

After a few moments, he glanced at her. She patted his shoulder, as thankful as he was that their scare was over. But still she sat back on her knees and couldn't help but be puzzled. "I'm so sorry, Jake."

"For what?"

"Maybe I didn't clean as well as I should have. How did I miss those pills?" She glanced at the bag on the dresser, sick to her stomach at the thought of what might have happened. "Eli, where did you find that bag?" She needed to know.

After all they'd been through, Eli suddenly seemed eager to explain. "The girls were playing house, and I was the *daed*. And I saw that thing wasn't in all the way." He pointed to a finial topping the metal bedpost. "I took it off and I was going to fix it like you fix things, *Daed*."

At that, Jake got to his feet, striding over to the bed. "You took off this finial?"

"Uh-huh, and the bag was inside. I pretended I was bringing home food and gave it to Sarah to cook for us."

Jake unscrewed the finial and sure enough, he pulled off a piece of tape from the inside of the bedpost that had held the bag of pills in question. It was a bed he and Lily had had during their marriage. He'd moved it from the Keim house.

"Did you take off any other finial?" Jake's concern seemed to well up all over again.

"Nee." Eli shook his head rigorously.

She watched as Jake instantly began to move around the bed, unscrewing the rest of the finials. "Dear *Gott*, help me. I thought I found all the pills."

All the pills? He'd spoken the words under his breath, but still she'd heard them.

"Hannah." Eli tugged on her apron, pulling

her attention toward him again. "I'm thirsty." He swiped at his runny nose.

"Let me guess. You want some hot chocolate, too?"

His response was a grin that lifted her spirits as much as it lifted his lips.

"Jake, I'm going to take Eli downstairs for some cocoa, *oll recht*?"

Jake stood up from looking under the mattress and nodded. "Of course. Will you tell Beth and Caleb I'm sorry to cut the evening short? And I'm sorry for all your hard work, Hannah. I just don't think I can—"

She held up her hand. "Jake, it's fine. I understand." At least that part she understood. "Beth and Caleb will, too. Things don't always go as planned."

"Jah." He sucked in a breath and let out a heavy sigh. "Things don't always go as planned."

His eyes steadied on hers, and with that look she thought there was more he might have to say. But instead, he turned from her abruptly.

As she and Eli made their way down the stairs, she could hear Jake's footsteps overhead along with the clamor of drawers and closets opening and closing, as he continued his search.

After putting the children to bed, Jake descended the steps, not sure if he'd find Hannah still there. Since there was no sign of movement in the house, he assumed she must've headed back to the *dawdi haus* after cleaning up the kitchen. All was silent except for the fleeting crackle of burning firewood. All was dark, as well, except for the light coming from the fireplace and the glow of the moon filtering through the window.

He certainly couldn't blame Hannah for taking off. It had been a strange evening, indeed, he thought as he went over to poke the fire into submission. It had started well and ended well, but in between—

"Whose pills were those, Jake?"

Startled by the sound of Hannah's voice, he turned to see her sitting in the armchair, staring into the fire. Her cloak already on, she looked as if she'd intended to leave much earlier but hadn't.

"Please be honest with me," she pleaded.

Caught off guard, he collapsed into the chair alongside hers. More than anything, he wanted to be open and honest with her, but he couldn't find his voice.

"They were Lily's, weren't they?"

He couldn't make himself say the words. But then, he knew his silence would tell the truth on its own.

"I remember the days, weeks, before Lily passed," Hannah said softly. "I felt so distant from her. She felt distant from me. But I have to say, over the years of your marriage, it wasn't a feeling that was new. I mean…" Hannah paused to chuckle lightly. "Goodness, we were mighty close, the three of us, when we were younger. Silly me, I thought it'd be that way forever. Or at least that's what I'd hoped." She sighed. "But then your marriage changed things. And it took some time—" her voice lifted "—but I finally accepted that things had to change. You were raising a family, and I was helping *Aenti* Ruth and working at the shop…" Her voice trailed off.

He tried to think of how to reply, but then she spoke again.

"But I have to say, when you two first got married, there were times when Lily and I could still laugh, and she'd tell me things. But as the years went by… I don't know. It hurt me how things changed between us. She'd always been like a sister to me. But it almost felt like she wanted me to stay away more. So I did."

When it came to Lily, he knew exactly what Hannah was saying. From the time he and Lily had married, it seemed she started to pull back from him—from everything. Not that it was right, but then he'd concerned himself mostly with his work and the children.

"When she fell off the horse, after her shoulder surgery, they gave her painkillers," he said quietly. It was his turn to stare into the flickering flames. "You'd asked me about them, remember?"

He could feel Hannah glance over at him. "Of course I remember. I brought over soup when she was recovering—and, well, it doesn't matter what I brought. I saw the bottle and when I asked her about them, she said they were nothing. That they'd only given her a few to take. And when I asked you, you said the same. But I was worried because she—I don't know, she seemed strange."

"Her shoulder healed," he told her, "but her addiction to those pills devoured her."

"But why didn't you tell me?"

He held up his hands, feeling defeated all over again. "She kept promising she'd stop. And for the *kinner*'s sake, I begged her to. But then I'd find more pills hidden in all kinds of places. And money missing, too. She'd hire an *Englisch* driver to take her to some *doktah* in a rural area not too far from here who'd sell her more."

"Is that how she died, Jake? From the pills?"

Right before Lily passed, she'd sworn that she was finished with the pills. For the sake of their children, he'd chosen to believe her. But the night he was startled by a thumping noise and woke up to find her missing from their bed, he knew for sure she hadn't been honest with him or herself. He found her contorted body lying at the bottom of the basement stairs, the life breath gone out of her. Everyone assumed the fall was a freak accident. Even though he discovered a stash of pills hidden in a box underneath the same steps she'd fallen from, for his children's sakes and their dead *mamm*'s reputation, he never said otherwise. Only her brother, David, knew the truth about what happened and wanted it kept quiet, as well. Not having heard from David for a long time, Jake was sure he blamed him.

"She died from the fall."

"Of course. But because of the pills?"

"She wouldn't want anyone to know that."

Hannah's head jerked. She was silent for a moment. "You know, Lily was the world to me. You both were." Her voice quivered. "But now I know what role I played. I was just 'anyone.'"

"Hannah," he huffed out her name. "You know that's not true."

How could she even think that when only days ago he'd told her how much she meant to him?

"Do I, Jake?"

Not giving him a chance to protest, she jumped up and dashed for the door, shutting it tightly behind her.

Chapter Ten

Oblivious to the never-ending bustle of the lumberyard, Jake fed another piece of white oak into the thickness planer, his mind still reeling from the dreadful events of the night before.

Hard as he tried, he couldn't suppress the bile rising in the back of his throat every time he thought about Eli's find and the harm that could've been done to him—and to his girls. Nor could he shake the anxious feelings reverberating through him as they had when Lily was still alive. Back when her addiction had taken over their home and lives. Back when he'd had to warn Sarah, who was barely four then, about the pills she'd discovered in Lily's apron pocket while trying to help him make soup for her listless *mamm*.

And now, to think what had happened the evening before could change his and Hannah's relationship tore at his very soul. To know that she was hurting…

Pain squeezed his heart as he recalled how they'd hardly glanced at one another when he'd left for work in the morning. As they'd crossed paths at the back door, they'd barely uttered a word.

Tormented, he grabbed another hardwood board and forcefully tossed it up on the machine. In doing so, he wished with all his might that life could be like a piece of wood that he could easily guide through a planer.

After all, hardwood comes from an oak tree that endures all kinds of conditions and a multitude of seasons, just like us, he mused. *Its trunk and limbs become marked and bruised. Yet in the end, the planer does its job. The wood gets sized just right, and each nick and blemish is stripped away.*

Engrossed in his thoughts, he lifted the finished board as it exited the planer, and rubbed his hand over its smooth, unmarred surface. As he did, he was reminded once again why he'd moved himself and his children. He'd hoped he would be rid of anything that tarnished his children's lives. He wished for a new future, a fresh start.

Yet, even being back in the house he'd grown up in, a place where he'd experienced happy memories, sometimes he couldn't sleep. He'd lay awake wrestling with his conscience, feeling remorseful about the way he'd handled Lily's problems.

Then Hannah had come along, and her presence had made such a difference in their lives. Truly, it felt as if everything around him had been cleansed, renewed. The *kinner*'s spirits were lightened. And the friendship the two of them shared seemed stronger than ever.

Until last night.

A tap on his shoulder jarred his thoughts. Turning, he saw Saul Hammond. Shifting his goggles to the top of his head, he pulled out his earplugs.

"Hey, Saul."

"You're whipping through those boards mighty quickly, Jake. Be careful," his coworker warned. "You don't want to scrape your hands or wrench your shoulder."

"I'm *gut*," he said, barely glancing Saul's way. He started to turn back to his work when Rosie suddenly appeared at their sides.

"You both need to join Seth in the break room," she said tersely without any of her usual banter or smiles.

"Is everything okay?"

"Head there now, please." She didn't seem able to look them in the eye. "I need to go tell the others," she added glumly.

He and Saul traded puzzled looks and then did as they were told. With so much on his mind about the previous evening and previous years, he couldn't imagine what Seth might say that could make him feel any worse.

Seth Hochstetler stood in the front area of the break room, looking like the leader Jake knew him to be. But a rare, painful expression was etched on his boss's face. No doubt, something was taking a toll on him.

"Good morning, ladies. Men." Seth nodded. "My news will, um…will only take a few minutes." He hesitated, before speaking in a low tone. "Some of you may have noticed that we're missing someone on the floor today. Tom McDaniel isn't here, and there is good reason for that."

Pausing to clear his throat, Seth continued, "Last night around midnight a fire broke out at the McDaniel home while they were all sleeping. Sadly, their house is pretty much gone. But more important, one of their children—Tom's seven-year-old daughter—was severely burned," he informed the group.

There were gasps all around the room. Jake was instantly sickened by the news. Tom's daughter, Katie, was close in age to his Sarah. From the stories he and Tom had shared, the two girls were alike in many ways. He couldn't imagine the horror Tom and his wife were going through.

"Katie? Is she *oll recht*?" he blurted.

"Katie was immediately airlifted to a hospital which is renowned for their burn care," Seth replied. "From all accounts, it sounds like she will be *gut*, given time. But, of course, the family has asked that we keep her in our prayers. They also asked for prayers for their other little ones. Their two boys weren't burned but are traumatized by the event and very frightened for their sister."

"Seth, would it be all right if we pray right now?" someone in the front row asked.

"Absolutely."

All around the room, the men and women bowed their heads, silently praying for the McDaniels. It was minutes before heads were raised and Seth began to share more.

"As I said, there was extensive damage to the family's home and their belongings. Tom did mention that his mother-in-law is widowed and was all set to sell her home and move into a nursing home. So, for right now they have a place to stay and may work out something with her. Regardless, I think you'd all agree that our community emergency fund should go to the McDaniel family at this time."

Everyone in the room murmured their agreement.

Seth nodded. "All right. Good. Rosie will personally deliver a check to Tom's family. Also, just to let you know, given the fact that Tom will be losing hours at work, we plan to help him out. Our company will compensate him the best we can. Our hope is that we can keep his position open for him. But, of course, we know that's asking a lot…" Seth looked around the room.

"We're happy to do the extra work until Tom gets back," one of the older men spoke up.

Heads nodded as unwavering shouts of *yes* and *jah* filled the room.

"I thought you all would feel that way," Seth said. "We're *verra* blessed to have such a great group of people here at Hochstetler's. *Danke.* Thank you all very much."

Rosie took the opportunity to stride up front alongside Seth.

"One last thing." She held up her index finger. "Just so you know, I'll be placing extra collection bins for Tom's family in the corner by our other bins." She pointed across the break room. "As always, Seth's mother, Mrs. Hochstetler, will be emptying the bins weekly and delivering your gift cards, small household items, clothes or whatever you'd like to donate."

As Jake went back to his spot at the planer, his legs leaden and his heart heavy, he made a pledge to himself that he'd be helping to fill those bins. Even so, that gesture of kindness wasn't enough to override the shame he felt.

He chided himself for being so lost in his own

concerns that he hadn't noticed his friend missing today. Not only that, he'd also been too wrapped up to stop and thank *Gott* for all the good he did have in his life. Starting with the Lord's unshakable, undeniable love.

It might've been years ago, but it felt like only yesterday that he had begged Lily to stop taking the pills. When she wouldn't, not knowing what to do and wanting the situation to go away, as wrong as it was, he'd scolded her. He'd told her she needed to pray harder. He'd said *Gott* couldn't hear her because she wasn't praying hard enough to be free of the disease that had overtaken her.

Now he needed to take his own advice. He needed to pray harder. Not just for his own life, but also for the others *Gott* had placed in his life.

Hannah was about ready to take the *kinner* over to the main house and start dinner when Jake walked into the *dawdi haus*. His face showed every bit of strain and sadness that Hannah imagined it would. As if the prior evening hadn't been enough, he had to be agonizing about his friend's tragedy, and that broke her heart for him. When Beth had stopped by after her shift to let Hannah know about the McDaniels, she'd been filled with worry for all of Tom's family, too.

Barely glancing her way, Jake immediately strode over to Sarah, who had been playing school with the twins. Removing the blackboard from her grasp, he knelt and pulled Sarah toward him. He hugged her tight.

When the twins saw how their father was acting, Hannah knew they had to be confused. This wasn't the playful dad they knew. Jake beckoned Clara and Eli to come close. He opened his arms and brought them into his embrace, nestling his head against theirs.

After hearing about Katie's injuries, when her eyes fell on any one of the children, she'd wanted to hold them close, too. She'd felt so overwhelmed with gratitude, knowing they were well and safe.

Still, she had to turn away and pretend not to notice Jake's intense display of love. Otherwise, she'd turn into a sobbing mess. Even *Aenti* Ruth, who was typically focused on her embroidery, was looking out the window, dabbing at her eyes.

As Jake pulled away from his children, he tugged a white bag from his jacket pocket.

"I know it's close to suppertime." He gave Hannah an apologetic glance. "But I brought home a treat for the *kinner*."

"Chocolate-covered pretzels!" Eli shouted and the girls were all smiles.

"It's fine by me," Hannah said.

As the children eagerly settled in at the table with their pretzels, Jake came over and touched her arm. "Can I talk to you, please? Outside?"

She nodded, and noticed Jake looked as relieved as she felt. Knowing her aunt would keep a watch on the children, she grabbed at the nearest warm thing, a thick shawl draped across a chair. Wrapping it around her shoulders, she followed Jake out to the porch.

The cold air instantly ran a shiver up her spine. Even so, she was glad to finally have a chance for them to talk. The day had felt endless as she'd waited for Jake to come home.

"Any more news about Katie?" she asked.

Not only had she heard Jake talk about the McDaniel family often, but she'd also met Tom and Ashley a few times when all the children had gotten together to play kickball before the weather turned colder.

"Nothing since I left work." He drew in a long breath and let out an equally long sigh.

"I'm so sorry to hear about them. It's awful."

"I know. All day long, I couldn't stop thinking about things. There's a lot I want to explain, Hannah."

"Jake." She laid a hand on his forearm. "It's not important."

He laid a hand over hers, intently staring into her eyes. "*Jah*, it is, Hannah. I need you to know that when all that was going on with Lily, I felt torn. I was trying not to betray her wish to keep things private. At the same time, I wanted to protect you from what was happening. I kept hoping that everything was going to work out and that you'd never have to know." He squeezed her hand. "But how I handled things was wrong in so many ways. Because of what I did—or more like didn't do—everyone got hurt, including you. I can't tell you how sorry I am, and—" His voice cracked. "Hannah, there can't be a wall between us. I can't lose you, too."

"You won't, Jake. You can't." She gently caressed his cheek. "Like it or not, you're stuck with me. Things changed years ago between the three of us, and I needed to accept that, and I have." She meant every word. "Although I have to tell you, last night…" She hesitated, not sure how much she wanted to share.

"Last night what?"

She shrugged. "I kind of felt orphaned all over again when I heard things about my two best friends in the world that I never knew. It made me feel the same loneliness I had when I lost my parents. And like maybe the relationships we had weren't everything I thought they were."

"I hate to think of you feeling that way."

"I know, and I don't anymore. I mean, it took some praying, crying, and lots of feeling sorry for myself. But then I realized that wasn't the only thing that was making me hurt so much."

"I think I can guess… You were also hurting

because you hadn't been there to help Lily. Trust me, Hannah. I have felt like that way more times than you know."

"But, Jake, you know what I realized?" She forced confidence into her voice. "I reminded myself that Lily was strong-willed, with a mind of her own. There wasn't much telling her what to do or how to do it, was there? Not about anything." Even though sadness gripped her heart as she thought of Lily being gone, a loving smile touched her lips when she thought of how she lived. "Even her *daed* shook his head at her time after time, and Lily and her *mamm* bickered constantly."

"*Jah*, they did clash often," Jake agreed.

"And pretty much always about nothing."

Jake chuckled. "I'm sure you're right."

"Lily's outgoing, impulsive personality drew some people to her, but it's also what hurt her and those around her. It had to be hard on you, Jake, living with lies. That's not you and deep down it wasn't Lily, either."

His jaw tightened in a flash. "She suffered with guilt, that's for sure."

"Guilt about the pills?"

"And other things," he said softly. "Even our decision to get—"

Hannah held up her hand, stopping him. "You know what? I don't want to know. Whatever went on in your marriage was between you two. It wasn't any of my business then and shouldn't be my business now. I just want to remember the three of us the way we were." She sighed. "That was a *verra* happy time in my life."

"Mine, too." He nodded, yet still looked troubled. "So, Hannah, will you forgive me?"

She felt humbled by his concern. "*Jah*, if you'll forgive me. I shouldn't have shunned you this morning. I felt bad the minute you stepped out the door."

"But, Hannah, you—"

She placed a finger on his lips. "No, let me finish. When I saw your *kinner* this morning, I felt even worse. It was then I realized how shallow I'd been. More important than anything I'm feeling are your children's feelings. Their well-being is crucial. By *Gott*'s grace they seem fine, and you've done a good job, Jake, of keeping them safe and happy. They never have to know about their *mamm*'s demons." She straightened herself, feeling stronger. "They only need to remember the way she loved them. And I promise, I'm going to do everything I can to make sure they remember her. We're going to make big, fluffy desserts and plant wildflowers in the spring, the kind Lily loved. And, *Gott* willing, I hope to find you a match who will love them like her own."

Jake stood staring at her, making her wonder

if she'd said too much. But she had to. It was everything that was on her heart.

Suddenly, he took both of her hands into his gentle clasp. "*Danke*, Hannah."

"For what?"

"For being you."

Hearing his sweet words, she felt her cheeks heat. Quickly she tried to change the tone of the serious moment. "Just remember you said that when a group of women shows up here on Saturday."

"I already know what you're going to say." He grinned. "When I stopped at the grocery store for the pretzels, I ran into Anna Graber. I'd forgotten her husband works with Ashley, so she knew all about the McDaniels' situation. She said you ladies are planning to cook and bake lots of things for Ashley to store away."

"*Jah*, Anna will be coming to help me and *Aenti* Ruth, along with Beth and Beth's mom, since the McDaniels' house was close to them. Marianne and Catherine from the bakery know the McDaniels, too, and they'll be helping out."

He winced.

"Don't you worry." She chuckled, patting him on the shoulder. "Catherine won't bother you. I promise. I took care of that. I mentioned to Anna that Catherine would be a *gut* match for Thomas Lehman. So now they're courting."

"You're right. I can see that. Those two can talk each other silly."

"Exactly." She nodded primly. "So we women will be cooking and baking, and it's perfect since we have two kitchens."

"Following in your footsteps, before I left town, I got a group of men to come over, too," he told her. "So many men that we'll probably be tripping over one another. We're planning to make bunk beds for the boys. It's something Tom had been talking about a while ago."

"And for Katie?"

"A bed, as well. A lot of their furniture was burnt up in the fire. And I think new beds may be comforting." He scratched at his beard. "I'm not certain of the design for Katie's yet, but it needs to be very special for Tom's princess. That's what he always calls her."

"I'm sure you talented men will come up with plenty of *wunderbaar* ideas."

"We hope to."

He paused, and even though the sun was setting, and a cool wind began to swirl around them, the way he gazed into her eyes warmed every part of her heart.

"Thank you, Hannah," he said, sounding just as sincere and heartfelt as he did before.

"For what?"

It took him a moment to answer.

"For helping me find my way. For helping me get back to being me again."

"Ah." She quirked a teasing brow, her best defense in slowing her rapidly beating heart. "And that's a *gut* thing?"

He pretended to be perturbed. "You know, you're not getting any pretzels if you don't start behaving yourself."

She waved a hand. "The *kinner* have probably eaten them all anyway."

They both glanced in the window, and she was sure he was as buoyed as she was to see his children enjoying themselves.

"True." He laughed. "Very true."

Chapter Eleven

Hannah stopped stirring another pot of beef stew being made for the McDaniel family just long enough to glance out the fog-streaked kitchen window.

"I feel bad being in this cozy kitchen while the men are working in Jake's cold barn," she said.

"I wouldn't worry." Anna chuckled. "I'm sure they're passing plenty of hot air between them, figuring out who's doing what to get those beds made."

"Thankfully, we're as organized in your kitchen as we are at Kauffman's." Beth held up a chef's knife triumphantly.

It was true, Hannah thought. The three of them were like a well-oiled machine, easily working together to make potpies, soups and stews for Ashley to freeze. They'd also already planned the supper they'd be cooking later to feed the volunteers at day's end.

"And it's a huge blessing the *kinner* are getting along just fine." Anna glanced into the other room, wiping her hands on the snug-fitting apron tied around her very pregnant belly. "I think that's mostly because Sarah has such a sweet way with them."

Before everyone arrived, Hannah hadn't been surprised when Sarah asked for help to make paper hearts, flowers and bears that she could have the twins and Anna's children color. Sarah thought it would make Katie and her brothers happy to receive cards from them.

"I think she's used to being in charge," Hannah told her.

The very thought saddened her some. More than once, Jake had also shared his dismay about how Sarah continually tried to step up and help.

If her dream had to be taken from her, Hannah was at least glad *Gott* had put her in a place where she might be doing another kind of patchwork and mending. She tried to do all she could to make sure Sarah got attention from her and Jake, as well. That was why she attended to the everyday things so Jake could have more time to spend with his children.

"Maybe I'll hire her to watch my *kinner*." Anna sounded excited about the prospect.

"I don't know, Anna," Hannah spoke up. "Sarah's too young to be alone with your *kinds*."

"No doubt about that," Anna agreed. "But if I

had Sarah there in the house with me, I could be free to do something else. You know, something fun—like laundry."

They all laughed at that.

"I guess in some ways I'm fortunate," Beth said as she passed a cupful of chopped onion to Anna. "By the time I have any *kinner*, Sarah will probably be old enough to tend to a baby. Or even old enough to have one of her own." She scowled at her own statement.

"Oh, now, Beth, it may be sooner than you think," Hannah assured her.

"I'm praying that's true." Beth sighed longingly. "*Gott* does have a funny way of doing things. Like having a person whom you've known all your life come into your life again and seem brand-new to you."

Her words caught Hannah off guard. Not that they should have. Hadn't that been her plan? For old friends like Beth and Jake to discover a new love between them? Still, the idea that it was happening for real tugged at her heart in a strange way. She swallowed hard, trying to think of a reply when Anna spoke up, talking about something altogether different.

"I'm glad we're doing this," Anna said, holding an unbaked potpie in both hands. Hannah scooted out of the way so Anna could slide the glass dish into the oven. "I can't stop thinking what it would be like if the same thing happened to one of our *kinner* like it did with Katie."

"I feel so sorry for them," Beth said softly. "They're such a sweet family."

Fortunately, they had learned that Katie would be all right. Eventually. The worst burn she'd received was on her arm. It had been so severe it required a full thickness graft and at least a two-week stay in the hospital along with more recovery time at home.

"Speaking of sweet," Hannah said, "it's kind of Catherine to head up the baking projects in the *dawdi haus*."

"They've got a good group over there," Anna replied. "Catherine, Marianne, your *aenti* Ruth and Beth's mom. And Abram, too."

"He's a funny man." Beth chuckled.

"You mean funny as in odd," Hannah stated.

Beth's brows furrowed. "*Nee*, I mean funny. I've only seen him a few times at Kauffman's, but every time I do, he makes me laugh. Like the other day when he was there with your *aenti*—"

"They were together at Kauffman's? I didn't know they went out to eat," Hannah interrupted. "I thought they were running errands."

"Maybe their errand was to have a romantic breakfast." Anna batted her lashes.

"Anyway," Beth continued, "he told a joke that had me smiling all day."

"Abram? Abram Mast did this?" Hannah couldn't believe her ears.

"Would your *aenti* have been with any other Abram?"

Beth and Anna looked at her as if she was the odd one.

"Well, no. It's just…he hardly ever speaks… to me." She frowned.

Had she done something wrong to quiet Abram? She couldn't imagine what. But then, she also couldn't imagine what her outgoing aunt had in common with him. And every time Hannah mentioned inviting someone like Joseph Beiler to dinner, her aunt would say she wasn't in the mood for company.

Staring out the window again, she wondered why she felt so unsettled. First, by the success of the match she did make, and then by the one she hadn't.

"Hannah?" Anna's voice sounded in her ears.

"Hmm?"

Her friend nodded toward the pot of stew, which had gone from simmering to boiling.

"Oh!" Hannah quickly turned down the heat. She needed to concentrate on what was right in front of her, and the things she could control.

Jake hesitated knocking on the *dawdi haus* door. It seemed like he was going courting or something. Although it was closer to bedtime than a respectable going-out time. Still, he couldn't wait to share his excitement.

Hannah opened the door tentatively. "Jake." She clutched her robe closed. "Is everything *oll recht*?"

"I just got the *kinner* to bed. They fell asleep quickly, but I'm all wound up," he admitted. "I thought we could take a walk, but I'm guessing you must be tired, too, ain't so? You worked hard today, cooking, cleaning, serving."

Hannah grinned. "When you say it like that, I should be more tired. But I haven't been able to settle down. I can't seem to turn off my mind."

He looked past her toward the sewing corner. "You lost a day of sewing, didn't you?"

"Jah." She let out a sigh. "I sewed for about an hour after everyone left, then told myself I needed to rest. But that hasn't happened. A walk might be a good distraction."

Elated, he grabbed her cloak from the rack, holding it open for her. She turned and he slipped it around her shoulders. "Where are we headed?" she asked.

"To the barn."

She laughed. "Oh, not a long walk, then."

"I'm sorry to say no," he apologized. "Honestly, I haven't been able to turn off my brain, either. I'm still excited about the work the men got done today. With everyone here past suppertime, then bedding down the children while you cleaned up, I never got to show you the beds we made."

The walk was quick as they strolled to the barn, the crescent moon lighting their way. Once inside, Jake quickly lit two lanterns. He noticed Hannah's eyes light up as soon as he handed her one.

"Oh, Jake." She rushed over to the closest piece of furniture, the set of bunk beds for the boys. "I can't believe the work you men did. It's incredible."

"I work with some very talented men," he felt proud to say. "And men from town dropped in all day long to help. We decided on a stair-loft bunk. We're thinking Michael, their oldest son, can climb the stairs to the top bunk. And Jeremy can have the bottom bed."

"Plus, it has two drawers they can use." She ran her hand over the wood and even pulled out a drawer.

"Some bunk beds have ladders, but we decided the boys should have a set of stairs instead. We wanted everything to be as safe as possible."

"After all they've been through, that makes perfect sense," Hannah agreed.

"And then for Katie…" He put an arm around her shoulder, leading her to the other end of the barn.

She gasped again, her eyes wide with wonder as she gazed at the bed they'd built for Katie.

"One of the men found a similar design online."

"It's like a play castle with stairs leading up to a twin bed on top."

"*Jah*, for Tom's princess."

"The children are going to love these new beds, Jake. They're more than beds. They're special places where they can feel safe again."

He'd been eager to show Hannah what had been accomplished, but he hadn't counted on how much her response would mean to him. Instead of feeling ten feet tall, he felt at least eleven.

"We had quite a team. We still have more some painting to do, but we're close to finishing."

"Do you mind letting me know when you'll be delivering the beds?" she asked. "I'd really like to make some shams and spreads."

"I was hoping you'd say that. More than once, Rosie has mentioned how ladies in town are talking about Hannah Miller's designs." He smiled at her. "You're making quite a name for yourself."

"Hannah Miller's designs?" She chuckled. "That's funny. Grace gave me a mountain of beautiful fabric, and I had to do something with it. Plus, *Aenti* Ruth is an embroidery whiz, which helps."

"Well, word has gotten out," he assured her.

"Rosie never stops talking about the pillow you made for her granddaughter's teacher. She said you came up with some saying on it about big hearts and little *kinner*."

"You mean 'It takes a big heart to shape little minds.' Trust me, Jake, that is not a new saying."

"It's new to me, and I thought it sounded very much like you."

"Are you trying to make me blush?"

He grinned. "It's not like I could tell in this light if you were." He paused. "Listen, Hannah, you have so many other projects on your plate. If you don't have time to make—"

"I want to very much," she interrupted him. "I'm not sure if I can do your woodworking justice, but I'll try. Like you, I'd like the McDaniel children to feel safe at night again."

Just then, Hannah yawned.

"Tiredness catching up with you?"

"*Jah*, but in a way, I don't want this day to end."

"I know what you mean."

"But you should get back to the house, Jake, in case one of the *kinner* wakes up."

"You're right."

Before exiting the barn, he extinguished the lanterns. They walked back to the *dawdi haus* in silence until they reached the porch.

"I can't thank you enough for arranging this day, Hannah." He paused to chuckle.

"What?" A curious smile curved her lips.

"I was thinking how you used to be the shy, quiet one in our group."

"Well, it was hard to compete with you and Lily. You were both quite outgoing and sure of yourselves." She defended herself.

"But things have shifted, don't you think? Now you're the town's matchmaker and popular seamstress. You've been my *kinner*'s lifeline and mine, too."

"You've been through a lot, Jake. It takes time to get yourself back on track. And when you think about the past, it all makes sense."

"What do you mean?"

She shrugged. "When we were young, you had the perfect family, people all around who loved you. You had every right to be sure of yourself. After losing my parents, I felt like I had to do everything right and keep in line for fear I could be orphaned again."

"Hannah, I never knew."

"And you didn't need to know." She laid a hand on his shoulder, once again making things easy for him. "Everything has worked out, Jake. I've learned to trust *Gott* will help me make it on my own."

"You've helped others make their way, too," he

told her. "In fact, I was thinking how the other day I thanked you for getting me back to being me. But I really should've thanked you for helping me be more like the person I want to be—and am trying to be."

She scrunched her forehead. "You mean caring and thoughtful of others?"

He nodded.

"But you've always been that person." She smiled, shaking her head. "Why, remember that time when Micah Stoltzfus was getting picked on by some *buwes*? You went right to his defense. You told the boys to stop and most of them did."

"All except for—"

"Willis Wittmer, who was the size of Goliath." She giggled. "Still you gave Wittmer a mighty big push."

"And thankfully he fell backward, knocked down a beehive and had bees swarming him." He laughed. "For a minute there, I was afraid Willis was going to get up and come for me."

"See? You've always been ready to help people, Jake." She gazed into his eyes, looking so earnest.

Right then and there, he wanted to tell her about Lily. The truth about why they married. It seemed like the perfect time. But it also seemed like it had been the perfect day, and he didn't want to ruin that. Or put an end to the way she was looking at him. After all, it had been a long time—many years in fact—since a woman he cared about looked at him so fondly. He had to admit, it felt *verra gut*. For the moment, he didn't want to put an end to that feeling, either.

Chapter Twelve

A couple of weeks later, Hannah had been sitting at her sewing machine since dawn, her Saturday just as busy as usual. She quickly realized that wasn't true for everyone.

"You're leaving, too?" she asked Jake, looking up from her sewing.

A half an hour earlier, Abram Mast had dropped by to pick up her aunt, saying they were going to take a buggy ride and maybe go shopping for a new board game. Well, Abram didn't exactly say that. *Aenti* Ruth had.

Now, here was Jake, saying he and the children were heading out, as well.

"Are you sure I can't fix breakfast before you go?" she offered.

"No need." He smiled. "I'm taking the children to Kauffman's. We haven't been there for a while."

Kauffman's Kitchen. Where Beth worked.

"Besides, you don't need to be cooking." He pulled gloves from his pocket. "You need to get your sewing done."

He was right, of course. News of her custom-designed, handcrafted decorative items kept spreading. Her client list had practically doubled, and with the holidays coming up, so had her workload. Busier than ever, after watching the children each day, she had been staying up, sewing late into the night.

"Oh, before you go, when do you want to take the shams and bedspreads over to the McDaniels'? I have the boys' linens done," she told him. "And I plan to finish everything for Katie's castle bed today."

In a way, she hoped it would be soon. She'd been missing having free time with Jake and the *kinner*. Beyond that, Jake said Tom had stopped by the lumberyard midweek to thank everyone for everything and to let them know Katie was back home. They'd moved into the house he and Ashley had purchased from his mother. Hearing that, some *Englischers* from Hochstetler's had rented a truck to haul the newly made beds to the McDaniels' new place the day before.

"How about we go after worship tomorrow?" Jake suggested. "Will that give you enough time?"

"That'd be perfect." She could feel her mood

instantly lighten. "I'll see you and the *kinner* in a little while, then."

"Probably not until late today." Jake tugged on a glove. "Beth's shift ends early, and we're taking the *kinner* to her cousin Bridget's house after she gets off. It'll be good for them to play outside with her cousin's children and wear themselves out."

She couldn't deny the way her heart involuntarily sank at his news. Her heart obviously hadn't come to terms with what her brain already knew—that Jake and Beth were the perfect match. Obviously, the two of them must be thinking the same.

Even though the dinner she'd initiated with Beth and Jake and Caleb hadn't ended well, apparently it had been the beginning of something good. Ever since, Beth and Jake had been seeing each other regularly. And hadn't that been her wish—to have a woman in Jake's life who would love him and his children wholeheartedly?

Her heart really needed to get a grip.

She swallowed hard. "I'm sure the children will love that." She took a moment to think. "Well, then, I'll have supper ready when you get—"

Before she could finish, Jake laid a hand on her shoulder. "Hannah, stop. We have plenty of leftovers. You just keep busy. We can bring over food to you later if you get hungry."

"*Jah*, okay, I'll do that. I'll keep busy," she heard herself say. "And you go have a *wunderbaar gut* time."

"We will."

She was quite sure he would. Plopping his hat on his head, he was out the door in an instant, appearing quite happy to be on his way.

Meanwhile, it took a minute before she could refocus on sewing the last seams on Katie's pillow shams. Even then, her mind kept drifting, imagining how well Jake and Beth must be getting along.

Her heart and mind weren't in sync, though. Because while happy feelings for the two of them flitted through her, she couldn't dismiss the pangs of jealousy poking at her. Which was odd. When she'd fixed up Jake with Miriam and Catherine, she'd never experienced such a roller coaster of emotions.

The realization thrust her out of her chair.

Yanking open the cabinet door, she began to sift through the yards of material, looking for fabric to match Katie's pillow shams. And a way to concentrate on something besides what she knew to be true.

Maybe a pastel floral for Katie's bedspread? Or just a light pink trimmed in lavender?

Yes, a pink to complement the pink crown topped with lavender hearts on the shams would work just fine, she decided. She started to lift the material from its spot, but then stopped. Instead, her hand seemed to have a mind of its own, running along the smooth wooden shelf…and remembering.

The day she'd gone to Sew Easy for the last time had been a bittersweet trip. Saying goodbye to Grace and farewell to her dream had been painful. Yet she'd also been blessed with her first freelance job. On her way back to the *dawdi haus*, she hadn't known whether to feel happy or sad. Then, when she discovered the beautiful cabinet Jake had made her, and when he had swung her around, so thrilled for her, all seemed right with the world again.

Her cheeks warmed at the memory; she wished she could go back to that simpler moment. Now she was happy for Jake and Beth, yet somehow, she couldn't deny a certain sadness, too. She could only hope that when Jake and Beth were living happily ever after, she could still be a part of their lives and the *kinner*'s, too. How she would miss sharing meals with them. Laughing together. Being there for them.

As tears pricked at her eyes, she hugged the piece of fabric to her chest. If only she didn't love them so, she wouldn't be so emotional about missing them already.

But you do love them. Sarah. Clara. Eli. She smiled, envisioning their sweet faces.

And Jake, too.

As a friend. She reaffirmed. *My best friend.*

Determined to keep her wavering heart on track, she paused long enough to take a deep breath. Then she shook out the fabric, straightened it and began measuring. She needed to stay focused on her work.

She needed to create something pretty and fit for a princess.

Beth had given Sarah and the twins way too many biscuits while they were at Kauffman's. Jake had been somewhat embarrassed about the drips of honey and blobs of jelly spread around the table. But the mess hadn't bothered Beth. She only smiled at their joyful faces and the way they enjoyed their treat. Like Hannah, Beth had always been easygoing and kind natured.

And though he'd never wish for anyone to go through what he had as far as a spouse dying, the fact that they'd both faced the same thing seemed to bond them closer. Even though they rarely spoke of their losses, their similar trials deepened the friendship they'd shared as *youngies*.

Older now, they could talk about pretty much

anything. The only problem was, as Jake leisurely guided the buggy out to her cousin's farm, the subject Beth most wanted to address was Hannah.

I've always envied Hannah." Beth sighed. "She certainly has a gift, doesn't she?"

"You mean her matchmaking?" He was sure that was what Beth was thinking of. Right before they'd left town, they'd run into Isaiah Glick and Amanda Shetler, a couple whom Hannah had matched up and who had recently announced their engagement.

Beth grinned. "I was thinking more about her sewing talent. But come to think of it, that's two things she's mighty good at. Matchmaking and creating beautiful items to grace people's homes."

Jake crooked his shoulder. "*Jah*, but like Hannah has told me, matchmaking and sewing are much the same. She takes pieces of material and sews them into a whole and brings a man and a woman together to make them a whole couple."

"That's Hannah for you, isn't it?" Beth sounded proud of her friend. "Humble as always."

"But she also thinks she's always right." His voice rose, unfortunately exposing his annoyance. Naturally, Beth instantly picked up on his frustration.

She snickered slightly. "Do you mean she

thinks she's right when it comes to knowing what's best for you?"

He nodded. "Mostly."

"Can you blame her?" She eyed him like he was a fool "You've known each other forever."

"But she may not be the matchmaker she thinks is," he bristled. "Her first two matches for me did not go well. Then she said they were only trial matches to get me back out into the courting world."

"Let me ask you this. Did she force you into those situations?" A knowing smile twitched at Beth's lips. "Because that doesn't sound like our Hannah."

"*Nee*, not exactly. I complained, and she made it sound like a solution for me and the children."

"Ain't so?"

"Yes, it is so." He frowned, wishing he'd never spoken his mind.

"That's interesting because I, for one, am not sure if you could ever find the right person, Jake."

"You mean, you don't know if Hannah can find the right person for me."

"*Nee*. You heard me right. I don't know if *you* can," Beth said matter-of-factly.

Slightly taken back, he jerked his head involuntarily. His grip loosened on the reins. "Am I that difficult to get along with?"

He wasn't sure if he wanted to hear her answer.

He already knew his past had made him stodgier. But he had every right to be. He wasn't the only one he needed to be concerned with. He glanced over his shoulder to see his children with their full tummies, looking content.

"I just mean it would be hard for you to get involved with someone, Jake, when Hannah is the one your heart wants."

He fell silent for a moment. "I said nothing of the sort."

She shook her head and clucked. "I don't know why you two didn't end up together when we were younger." She laid a hand on the arm of his jacket. "Please, don't take that the wrong way. I loved Lily. You know I did. But when I think of a perfect match, it's always been you and Hannah."

As much as he trusted Beth, there was no reason for him to share everything that had happened with him and Lily or his feelings for Hannah all those years ago.

"It wasn't meant to be," he said simply. "But I'm not sure matchmaking is for me, either."

He could feel her staring at him, and he knew her well enough to know she was sizing him up.

"Oh… I think I know what's happening here. You've asked me to run about with you and the *kinner* lately so Hannah will think we're a match." Her eyes sparkled with the realization.

"Well, *jah*, but…" He gave her a sideways

glance. "Really, Beth, hasn't it been nice keeping busy with us until Caleb moves back to town? And, haven't I been helpful checking out your beau's new store space with you and making remodeling plans?" He paused, happy to change the subject. "You have mailed those ideas to him, haven't you?"

"Of course I did. And yes, I've enjoyed the time with your family. But, Jake…" She looked away for just a moment. "Now you're making me a part of your deception with Hannah."

"Trust me, it's not any more deceptive than she's been." He could feel himself getting flustered again. "You're not as savvy to Hannah's ways as I am."

"Jake, Hannah is a sweetheart and you know it."

"*Jah*, she is. But also, a finagler."

"Hannah?" Beth giggled.

"It's true." His head bobbed decisively. "Remember that first dinner we all had together? I was supposed to be taking a break from matchmaking then, but I realized that Hannah was doing everything she could to push us together." He shook his head, remembering. "Even before you walked in the door that night, she was complimenting the blue shirt she'd ironed for me, telling me it was your favorite color."

"Blue is my favorite color."

"Exactly my point!" he exclaimed.

He glanced at her long enough to see her brows furrowed in thought. "What you need to know, Beth, is that it's not just about me and match-making right now. It's about Hannah. With you and me spending time together, we're letting her concentrate on the business she's growing. She's not one to put herself first, you know. Sewing and designing is what she likes to do best, and it's what she deserves to do."

"You have said she's been *verra* busy."

"Unbelievably. Her customers have been growing by leaps and bounds."

He'd been thrilled for Hannah, but also concerned about how worn out she'd been looking lately. So much so that he kept himself at a distance, knowing if he got too close, he'd want to reach out and massage her hunched-over shoulders or let her rest her head on his.

He even wished he could take a turn at the sewing machine so Hannah could put her feet up and rest for a bit. But that would be sure disaster and only cause her more stress. From the sounds of it, even Ruth wasn't much of a seamstress.

He had thought about suggesting that she should take a night off from sewing. After all, wouldn't it be good for her to spend an evening with him the way they used to? Relaxing. Reading. Talking. Sharing their day. But he never brought up the idea. He knew he'd only be asking her for selfish reasons. He missed ending his days that way.

"So you don't think I'm being deceptive, then?" Beth interrupted his thoughts.

"If you have, then you've made me part of your deception, too, Beth. Caleb's father was in Hochstetler's the other day and—"

"You didn't say anything about Caleb moving back, did you?"

"It almost slipped out," he admitted.

"Honestly, I've seen them at worship several times, and I've almost said something, as well." Her eyes grew wide. "We have to be careful. Caleb is really set on surprising his family."

"They'll be thrilled."

"So then, let's not say we're partners in deception. Let's say we're two friends helping each other and helping those we care about the most."

"That sounds *verra gut*," he agreed. "And true."

"I have to tell you, though…" Beth's voice turned somewhat giddy. "Caleb will be here full-time soon, and I'm thinking I won't have many free days then. I hope." She giggled, and even though she was on the other side of the seat, he could see her cheeks turn rosy. "Did I tell you? He's already asked me to help run the butcher shop with him."

"You two will make a great team."

Jake knew Caleb was planning on asking Beth much more than that, but he'd never say so.

"Once that happens, you may find Hannah trying to make a match for you again."

"When the time comes, I'll figure it out." He gripped the reins tightly knowing that day was coming soon. "Until then, I really do appreciate your help."

She nodded, and with that settled, he concentrated on the road again. Until Beth spoke up.

"I really hope you'll think about everything I've said. I really do want you to be happy. And you and Hannah are a perfect match."

He didn't say a word.

After all, if he and Hannah were so perfect for each other, why wasn't the matchmaker asking him to be *her* match?

Chapter Thirteen

Just as she and Jake had planned the day before, after worship Hannah made sure everything was stowed in the buggy, ready for their visit with the McDaniels. And most everything was—except for her.

The children had grand ideas about what they wanted to take to Katie McDaniel and her brothers—games, cookies and the cards they'd made. Yet as soon as Jake announced it was time to leave, they burst out of the house and climbed into the buggy, leaving all those items behind. Now Hannah stood with her arms full of their gifts, deciding the best approach for boarding the buggy herself.

"Need some help?" Jake was suddenly at her side.

"I'm thinking I do."

She started to hand him a couple of satchels until she realized Jake wasn't reaching for those. Instead, he was reaching for her. His hands hugged her waist, lifting her as if she and her parcels were as light as feathers. Then he settled her just as easily onto the buggy's seat.

"There you go." He smiled before rounding the buggy and getting in.

"*Jah*, there I go…again," she whispered to herself.

Because as soon as he settled onto the seat next to her and took the reins, the lingering feel of his hands made her feel light-headed. She couldn't stop from thinking of another time, a day in late summer when they were teens, walking and talking till nearly dusk. It had been just the two of them. Lily hadn't wanted to come along. They'd almost made it back home when they stopped, and Jake reached around her waist in the same way, hoisting her up so easily onto the stone wall that ran along the Klingers' property. There they sat side by side, watching the sun set, and she thought her heart would melt when he'd reached over, pulled her close and—

"I'm not a baby, Sarah," Clara began shouting. "I know what lions say. Stop asking me. They say *roar*. And I know what dogs say, too. They say *ruff-ruff*."

Hannah turned in time to see Clara grab the lion puppet from Sarah's left hand and the dog puppet from Sarah's right.

"Clara, that's not nice," Hannah reprimanded her. "If you'd like to use the puppets, you need to ask nicely."

"But they're *my* puppets." Clara hugged the cloth animals close, her lips in a pout. "You made them for me."

That was true. Clara had asked Hannah to make puppets, and Hannah had been glad to. She'd deliberately made the cutest lion and dog puppets she could.

Wanting to restore harmony, Hannah decided there was only one answer to give.

"I may have made them for you, Clara, but we're all supposed to share. And I'm not just talking to you, Clara. I'm speaking to you, Sarah and Eli, too. You are family," she reminded them, "and that's a *verra* special thing. Like I've told you before, you need to help each other and share. Just like you are sharing with others who aren't in your family." She held up one of the satchels in her lap.

The children were silent, their expressions serious. The only sound to be heard was the clip-clop of the horses' hooves and a squeak from Jake's seat when he turned to glimpse at his children. "Listen to Hannah. She's right."

"I heard you, Hannah," Clara said. "Here, Sarah." She kindly started to hand the lion puppet to her older sister.

"*Nee*, you keep it." Sarah smiled sweetly.

"I'll take it." Eli grabbed for the puppet.

"Eli!" Clara wailed, shaking her hand. "You hurt me and Leo."

Hannah had to bite back a chuckle. "I tried." She shrugged at Jake, who was staring at her with a strange look on his face. Usually she could easily read his expressions, but this time she couldn't.

"What?" she asked.

"It's just…you are…" He looked like there was something he wanted to say, but then dipped his black hat before quickly settling his eyes back on the road. "Thank you for taking such good care of them, Hannah."

She started to slough off his words and teasingly reply, "It's my job." But she couldn't, because it wasn't that simple. She also couldn't say, "Why wouldn't I? They're family." Technically, that was false, as well.

She plainly answered, "I'm happy to."

Less than ten minutes later, after passing Graber's Horse Farm, they arrived at the McDaniels' two-story home. Jake had warned the children earlier about being careful and not roughhousing around Katie. He reminded them once again as he pulled the buggy onto the acre-and-a-half lot, mostly eyeing Eli as he spoke.

As usual when they visited, Jake unhitched

the buggy and let the horse free in the fenced-in yard. After that, he went to work, retrieving the plastic bags of bedding from a rear trunk while she and the children walked to the front porch and rang the doorbell.

Ashley opened the door, with Jeremy, her two-year-old, hugging her leg, and a shy-looking Michael gripping the hem of her caramel-colored sweater. Then there was Katie, who stood back, appearing nervous about getting too close.

This certainly wasn't the outgoing group of kids Jake's children had played with just a few weeks before the fire. Clara, however, broke the ice right away, pulling her dog puppet from behind her cloak.

"Hi. My name is Biscuit." She wiggled the puppet, and Hannah could tell she'd tried to come up with a puppy's voice. But the sound was still all Clara's, sweet and peppy, bringing curious smiles to everyone's faces.

"That's a nice name, Biscuit," Ashley said.

"I like biscuits, so I like you, too, Biscuit." Clara's four-year-old peer let go of his mother's sweater and stepped forward.

"Do you like jelly on your biscuits?" Clara waved the puppet, as if it was doing the talking.

"Lots of jelly." Michael nodded.

"Me, too," Clara exclaimed.

With that, all the children seemed to relax

more. When Jake reached the porch, his arms full of bags, Michael pointed to the largest one. "What's in there?"

Jake leaned toward the boy. "I've been told it's something out of this world," he said quietly, as if sharing a secret. Then he looked at Hannah and grinned. She knew Jake was referring to the boys' bedding, which she'd designed with stars and planets in mind. It warmed her heart when the boys' faces lit up with curiosity.

"Can we see, Mom?" Michael asked.

"We can if we move out of the doorway and let everyone in." Ashley chuckled.

The visitors removed their coats, and the Mc-Daniel kids got a good look at their new bedding. Then all the children happily settled into the family room, playing the game the Burkholder *kinner* had brought.

Hannah noticed Ashley didn't mind a bit that the six of them were getting cookie crumbs on the rug. Instead, as the men sat in a pair of leather recliners, Ashley offered Hannah a cup of tea.

"If I'm being honest, what I'd really like is to see how the bedding fits," Hannah told her.

"I was hoping you'd say that." Ashley grinned. "But I didn't want to put you to work."

Once upstairs, as Ashley pulled each item out of the bags, she oohed over every one of them, complimenting Hannah repeatedly. Working together, they quickly fit pillows into shams and smoothed out comforters over sheets. When they finished, Ashley was beaming with joy.

"Look at what you've done, Hannah!" she exclaimed. "Their rooms are perfect now. My kids can feel at home here. They'll want to be in their rooms again." Ashley's eyes began to grow misty. She reached up to touch the pink, white and lavender lace and chiffon garland Hannah had made to hang between the turrets on Katie's castle bed. "You really can't know how much this means to me. I'm so very thankful to you."

"It wasn't just me, Ashley. The beds the men built were a great inspiration—along with Tom's pet name for Katie." She smiled.

Ashley's chin quivered and her brows arched with sincere appreciation. "I don't know how I'll ever repay you—repay everyone—for the beds, the food and sweets, and the cards and kind thoughts. Plus, the donations from Hochstetler's haven't stopped. It's all so much!"

Hannah gently squeezed her friend's arm. "Everyone just wants the best for your family."

"How blessed Jake is to have you, Hannah. And the children are, too," Ashley said with the utmost sincerity.

"Jake and I, well, we're only friends."

"You mean for now," Ashley insisted. "Tom says Jake talks about you all the time at work."

"He does?"

"And very fondly." Ashley winked. "Why wouldn't he?"

Hannah started to tell Ashley about Beth, but her friend immediately jumped to a new subject—curtains for the children's rooms.

"I'll only allow you to make the curtains if you'll let me pay for them," Ashley told her.

"Fine, but I'll give you my 'friend' discount," Hannah countered.

"Oh, all right," Ashley agreed. "If that's the only way I'm going to get Hannah Miller curtains."

They began writing down window sizes and discussing colors and fabrics. But all the while, Hannah couldn't stop thinking about what Ashley had said.

Had Jake really been talking about her?

The longer Jake sat talking with Tom, the more uneasy his friend seemed. And the more stilted their conversation became. He wasn't surprised when Tom jumped up from his recliner the minute Ashley and Hannah came downstairs.

"I'd like to show Jake around the property," he informed his wife. "Sound good?" He eyed Jake.

"Sure." Jake nodded.

"No worries." Ashley told him. "We can manage kid duty. Can't we, Hannah?"

"Without a doubt." Hannah shooed them away.

With that, Tom threw on his coat and handed Jake his jacket so quickly that Jake figured the outing wasn't only about exploring Tom's new homestead.

He was right.

"Sorry," Tom apologized as soon as they were outside. "Sometimes I just have to get out of there. It's like I can't breathe. I look at Katie and how timid my boys have become and my heart breaks." He ran a hand through his thick hair.

Jake started to ask how he could help, when Tom abruptly pointed to a level spot in a far corner of the yard past where Jake's horse had settled in.

"This spring, that's where I'm putting a shed for lawn equipment."

"Makes sense." Jake nodded.

"I always wondered why Ashley's dad didn't have a place to store lawn gear. Right now, it's cluttering half the garage."

"Jah," Jake agreed. "When I moved, there were a few things about my parents' property that I thought could be better. I guess in our line of work, we're always looking for ways to make improvements."

Jake thought he sighed heavily at times until he heard Tom exhale. "Yeah, well. I wish I had thought of making some before the fire. Like rope ladders, for one."

Jake winced, his heart as heavy as it was when he'd first learned about his friend's tragedy. "How is Katie doing?"

"She…she's…the sweetest." Tom's voice cracked. "She tries to act like she's doing fine. But I know she's in pain. I know she still has bad dreams. The boys do, too. But they tell me about them. And Katie? My princess won't say anything because she doesn't want to worry us."

"Our girls are very much alike." Jake clasped his friend's shoulder. "It kills you, doesn't it?"

"So much." Tom dipped his head. "And then Ashley…whew…" His lips tightened. "Sometimes I can barely look at her. What kind of husband and father am I? Because of me, she almost…" He exhaled. "She almost lost her babies."

He turned away. Jake could tell he was swiping at his eyes, trying to get a hold on himself. It took a minute before Tom circled back around. "How could I have been so *stupid*?"

From what Jake had heard, the cause of the fire wasn't a rare case. Tom had drifted off while in his recliner, studying the roster and playbook for Katie's basketball team. Unfortunately, those papers had fallen to the floor near a space heater that he'd forgotten to turn off before heading to bed. It was a simple mistake that had turned devastating.

"I think there are always things we wish we could've done differently." Jake certainly knew that to be true.

"I've scarred everyone I've ever loved the most." Tom threw his arms up in the air. "And I can't stop blaming myself. I don't think I ever will." He gnashed his teeth, staring out into the yard.

"You know, when you'd tell me what you were going through with Lily," he continued, "I remember saying that you shouldn't blame yourself. That sometimes life takes turns that you never expected." He shook his head disgustedly. "I must have sounded callous."

"I didn't really expect you to have all the answers."

"Well, now I have a way better understanding of what you were going through. Unfortunately. The guilt is tearing me up, man. I feel like… I couldn't be a worse father."

A sob erupted from deep within Tom's chest. Jake reached out and clasped him around the shoulders, feeling the clutches of sorrow grab at him, as well.

He cleared his throat. "Tom, you can take some time to be sorry. But then you must get past it. You have a *wunderbaar* wife. *Wunderbaar* kids.

Don't let yourself get lost to them. They deserve all of you."

When Jake looked at his own children, it was something he'd had to remind himself again and again. And still did.

Tom buried his head in Jake's shoulder, weeping. Jake patted his friend's back. "Turn to *Gott*. He will forgive you," Jake told him. "He is a *Gott* of second chances. He will heal your heart and give you a new spirit to go forward. That's His promise."

He hoped Tom believed it for himself and the ones he loved. He wished he could believe it, too. As much as he knew *Gott* was a forgiving *Gott*, he still had a hard time completely forgiving himself.

Tom stepped back and wiped at his cheeks.

"I'm grateful to you, buddy," Tom told him. "I mean it. And you know, I have to tell you, you look better to me. And seeing you and Hannah together…" He paused. "It does give me hope."

Jake started to object but then stopped. Was that Tom's voice he was hearing or was *Gott* whispering in his ear?

Chapter Fourteen

❧

The weeks had been passing by quickly. Each day had, too. Hannah had just finished reading time with the children when Jake's buggy pulled into the drive. His timing was perfect as usual. Or maybe she should take a little credit where credit was due, Hannah thought, grinning inwardly. Once again, she'd scheduled the day's activities with the children just right.

"Grab your coats, *kinner*! Your *daed* is home from work. And don't forget the kitty treats we made," she added. "They're in a paper bag by your boots."

"It's my turn to carry the bag," Eli informed his sisters.

Hannah noticed neither sister wasted a minute arguing. Instead, they were all sticking to what had become their new habit.

With winter coming closer to an end and more

daylight to be had each day now, they eagerly donned their jackets like clockwork and romped outside to greet their father. Each day, too, she'd gaze out the window with a fond smile.

Jake might've been tired from his day at work, yet no one would ever guess it. He'd welcome the *kinner* with open arms and take his time lifting each of them into the air, beaming joyfully all the while. Then the children would grab Jake's hands, skipping happily into the barn.

As Hannah watched them disappear into the stable to feed the kittens, more and more each day it seemed like a sign of things to come. Certainly, as time went on and Jake and the children grew even closer to Beth, things were apt to change. Then would she even be needed? The realization tugged at her heart.

Sighing wistfully, she pulled from the refrigerator the ground-beef-and-noodle casserole that she'd prepared earlier in the day. Placing the dish into the heated oven, she was about to start making biscuits, when a knock sounded at the front door.

Quickly, her mind rifled through her list of deadlines. But she came up with what she already knew—it was only Thursday. No orders were due until Monday.

Still, assuming the visitor might be a client, she hurriedly tucked wispy hairs into her *kapp*, wiped her hands on a dish towel and headed toward the door.

Shooting a curious glance out the picture window, she saw a shiny red sports car in the arc of the driveway. It was a car she surely would've remembered if she'd ever seen it on the roads of Sugarcreek. As she opened the door, she realized the *Englisch* woman standing there didn't look familiar, either. Clad in a fancy white wool coat with a fur collar, the lady appeared as if she'd just stepped out of a magazine. She wore pointy-toed black boots and brown leather gloves and hugged a glossy mocha-colored purse to her side.

"Hello." The stranger removed a glove, extending her right hand. "Are you Hannah Miller?" Fortunately, her smile was far more down-to-earth than both her automobile and clothing.

"*Jah*, I am." Hannah rubbed her hands on her apron to make doubly sure they were clean before taking the attractive woman's hand.

"The same Hannah Miller who made the decorative pillows for Julie Caples?—who is my sister-in-law, by the way. And also bedding for the McDaniels, the stool cushions for Kauffman's Kitchen, and the adorable swaddles for Sylvia Wright's new granddaughter?" The woman barely paused before adding, "Yes, I've done some snooping around town and know you have several more satisfied customers. But I suppose I don't need to list everything I've heard about and seen of your work."

"Jah." Hannah blinked. "That would be me."

"Good, I'm in the right place, then." The woman released Hannah's hand. Deftly taking a business card from her purse, she gave it to Hannah. "I'm Madeline Enyart."

Giving the pink-and-gold card a swift glance, Hannah slipped it into her apron pocket. "Nice to meet you. Would you like to come in?"

From the moment Madeline stepped inside, Hannah could see she was scanning the sitting room, eyeing the pillows, cushions and window dressings Hannah had made.

"Everything looks so warm and inviting in here," her new acquaintance commented. "And those are darling."

Madeline pointed to the smaller rocking chairs that Hannah had recently encouraged Jake to purchase for the children. She thought it was time they had their own reading chairs. She had sewn cushions for the chairs and in the middle of the back cushions, she had added a square of fabric with a blessing printed on it.

"Danke. And is there anything I can make for you?"

"I certainly hope so." Madeline Enyart's chuckle was a pleasant sound. "Hannah, I'd like to tell you about myself—well, my business actually. I have an interior design studio in Columbus called Decor to Adore, and it's doing quite well. So well, in fact, that I'm opening another studio in Sugarcreek. The thing is—" she paused to remove her other glove, as if getting down to business "—I've been successful using outside companies and seamstresses to create our products. But from what I've seen of your work, there's a warmth, and interestingly, a brightness to your designs that's rare. Just like in this room." She waved her gloves theatrically in the air. "That's why I'd like for you to come work with me."

Hannah squinted, trying to comprehend what Madeline was saying. "You mean do some work for you."

"No, I mean be involved in a partnership with me," Madeline said definitively, raising her brows. "Your work could be in so many homes and delighting so many families, Hannah. And not just in Sugarcreek. Think of all the tourists who come to this town." Her eyes grew wide with excitement. "Decor to Adore, featuring Hannah Miller Designs. It really has a special sound to it, don't you think?"

Stunned beyond belief, Hannah didn't know what to think. Could this really be happening?

* * *

"That's a *verra* red car, *Daed*," Eli noted, the minute Jake and his *kinner* exited the barn.

"*Jah*, it is, *sohn*."

Jake wasn't surprised to see an *Englischer*'s car in his driveway. Automobiles were no longer an unusual sight on his property with Hannah's customers coming and going, picking up their purchases. He'd even been happy to make a few deliveries himself from time to time. As much as Hannah helped him, he wanted to return the favor whenever possible.

"Why aren't buggies a pretty red like that car?" Clara frowned.

"She's right, *Daed*," Sarah chimed in. "If our buggies were red then cars and trucks would see them better."

Though the children had a point, Jake was about to explain how the Amish way was more reserved, when Ruth opened the *dawdi haus* door.

"What have you *kinner* been doing today?" Ruth called out to them, steadying her wheelchair. "I've missed you. Do you have time for a visit?"

"May we, *Daed*?" Sarah asked politely, as always.

"I'll bring them over when dinner's ready," Ruth offered.

"That sounds *gut*, Ruth. *Danke*."

It sounded better than good, actually. While the children scampered into the *dawdi haus*, Jake headed directly home, like a man on a mission. After he washed up for dinner, and Hannah's customer left, he hoped he might have time alone with her.

In the weeks since visiting the McDaniels, he'd been thinking plenty about what Tom had said. If he was being honest, he'd noticed changes in himself, too.

Consequently, he'd been diligently praying, asking for *Gott*'s forgiveness along with seeking guidance where Hannah was concerned. He hadn't exactly heard *Gott*'s voice, but things between him and Hannah seemed more intensified than ever.

The glow of her smile warmed him from across the room. The sound of her laughter lifted his heart, moving him to join in. And when they'd share a look across the supper table, or while playing with the children, or simply saying goodnight, he felt as if they were connected more than ever.

Now he wanted to know if she felt it, too.

Slipping in the back door quietly, he didn't want to disturb Hannah and her customer. Typically, he ignored the women's conversations, figuring they were about things he had no knowledge of or little interest in, like thread counts.

But this conversation struck him differently, sounding more serious. He knew he shouldn't eavesdrop, but he leaned against the wall, listening in.

"So, Hannah," the lady was saying, "would you consider moving back to town and working together? I've purchased a house that will become the design studio, and there's a great little house that I bought right next door. You can live there at a very reduced rate so you can be on hand to consult with clients."

"That's the only way I could come work for you?" Hannah asked.

"Not *for* me," the visitor corrected Hannah. "With me."

"But couldn't I just ride into town whenever you need me?"

"How would you know when I need you?"

Jake was curious about Hannah's answer.

"There's a phone shanty across the street," Hannah replied. "That's helped a lot with the business I'm doing now."

He heard the woman sigh. "It's not the arrangement I'd hoped for. Besides, I hear you're a nanny for Mr. Burkholder's children. When on earth do you have time to sew?"

"I make time," Hannah stated. "At night and on Saturdays."

"I can't imagine you have much time to stop and breathe. And whether you take on a partnership with me or not, I'd be careful about that," the lady advised. "I'm not trying to sound like a know-it-all, but at the rate you're going, it could eventually take a toll on your health and your creativity."

As much as Jake didn't want to take this stranger's side, he also couldn't imagine how Hannah could keep up her pace.

"I haven't been late with a delivery yet." He heard Hannah defend herself.

"And you've truly created some beautiful items," the woman complimented Hannah. "That's why I'm here, and why I'm hoping you'll form a partnership with me. It just requires a simple move to town." Her voice lightened. "Not a trip to the moon or anything." She giggled slightly. "So, please think about it, will you, Hannah?"

Hannah said something softly, but he couldn't hear what.

"I hate to lose you, so I'll be doing some thinking, too," the visitor continued. "The builders are finishing up remodeling work on both houses. So there's still some time, but not much. I'll reach back out to you, and you have my card if you need to contact me."

As the women exchanged goodbyes, Jake knew

he should move quickly and act like he had just come inside. He didn't want Hannah to think he was spying on her.

But in his heart of hearts, after what he'd heard—as hard as it was to hear—he felt pressed to address Hannah's opportunity. He stood frozen to his spot.

"Jake!" Hannah jumped when she saw him. "How long have you been in the kitchen?"

"Sorry to surprise you like that," he apologized. "Did I hear what I think I heard?"

She shrugged nonchalantly. "It was someone who needed work done."

"That's not the way I understood it."

She started to walk around him, and he caught her by the hand. "Hannah, what this lady is saying—it sounds like everything you've been working toward since Sew Easy closed."

Unable to contain himself, he took both of her hands into his. As much as he wanted to hold on tight and never let go, he squeezed them gently, encouragingly. "This is your chance to shine. An opportunity to be a partner in a design studio."

"It's nothing, Jake."

He could tell she was trying to muster up an indifferent expression, but her cheeks appeared as heated as the kitchen they were standing in. Clearly, she was flustered.

"Listen, Hannah, I shouldn't have eavesdropped. I realize you have every right to be upset with me."

"Who says I'm upset?" she asked innocently as if it was the furthest thing from her mind.

"Hannah, I know you, remember? Again, I'm sorry."

"I'm not upset with you, Jake."

"What is it, then?" He looked into her eyes, searching for a clue, but she deliberately let her eyes drift from his.

"It's just… I need to finish dinner for everyone." She slipped her hands out of his grasp. "And afterward, I need to finish sewing pants for Eli. He's growing out of everything these days."

He crossed his arms over his chest. She may have freed herself from his hands, but he was not about to let her brush him off so fast. For her own sake.

"You have to stop this," he said in a sharp tone.

"Stop what?"

"You know what," he insisted impatiently. "You have to stop being everyone's everything. For once, you need to think about yourself and what you want."

Hannah walked past him, headed toward the oven. "Right now, I smell the casserole burning," she quipped, obviously determined to cut the conversation short. "I just need to think about that."

Chapter Fifteen

When Hannah came into the house as he was leaving for work the next morning, it ran across Jake's mind that he'd probably laid eyes on her pretty face thousands of times. That was why, when he saw her hollow eyes and less-than-bright smile, he knew for sure she hadn't slept well the night before.

He could relate. He'd hardly slept himself.

The glimmer of moonlight that had filtered into his bedroom should've been soothing and restful, but instead it seemed to shine a light on everything that had to do with Hannah, leaving him restless. He literally ached, hating the thought of having things change and not having her close…and in his life. About the only time he'd closed his eyes was when he was trying to shut out thoughts of his children. They would be incredibly hurt by her leaving. How they would miss her!

Still, he had to do whatever he could that would be best for Hannah. Yet even after stewing all night, he wasn't sure what that was. And although the sun shone brightly throughout his entire ride to work, he sank into a deep trance. The monotone clip-clopping of the horse's hooves only magnified that feeling.

Thankfully, once he arrived at Hochstetler's, the hustle and bustle of the lumberyard had a way of energizing him. After an hour into his shift, with a plan in mind, he strode into his boss's office.

"Seth, do you have a minute?"

His boss looked up from his paperwork. "Sure, Jake. How can I help you?"

"Is there a way I can get in touch with your mother?"

"This is Friday, isn't it?"

Jake nodded. "Why, *jah*, it is."

"It's easy, then. She'll be here a little later to collect donations from the bins for her weekend deliveries."

"Does she usually stop by to see you when she comes in?" Jake asked.

Seth opened the top drawer of his desk enough for Jake to see baggies filled with cookies and treats. "Where do you think I get all of these?"

Jake chuckled. "Do you mind letting me know when she gets here? I really need to talk to her."

"*Jah*, I can do that," Seth replied. "Anything I can do in the meantime?"

"Only if you want to babysit my *kinner*."

Seth sniggered. "I'll be sure to let you know when *Mamm* arrives."

Two hours later, after a ten-minute talk with Seth's mom, explaining his situation and Hannah's opportunity, Jake had his answer. Mrs. Hochstetler not only assured him that she'd be happy to take care of his children while he was at work, but also offered to help him find a long-term solution. It was everything she had promised months earlier.

Knowing he could offer Hannah a solution, he figured he'd have a sense of relief. Rather, all throughout his shift, everything felt heavy inside him, from his heart down to his feet. He was still feeling that way at day's end when Rosie sauntered up to him at the time clock.

"You're looking at me funny." He swiped his badge to check out. "Am I doing something wrong?"

"I don't know. Are you?" Rosie asked.

"I'm not sure I know what you mean."

"Of course you do, Jacob. Don't play dumb with me."

He shrugged. "No one ever said I was the sharpest tool in the shed. Maybe the handsomest…"

He tried to make her laugh to get her off track,

since he figured she'd heard about the setup with Seth's *mamm*. But Rosie crossed her arms over her chest, not one to be easily distracted.

"I hear Mrs. H. is watching your kids so Hannah can move back to town. Is that true?"

"That's the plan. Until I find a long-term nanny." He tucked his badge into his shirt pocket. "Hannah has a great opportunity awaiting her. She needs a chance to do what's best for her."

"But do you think this is really the way to go?"

He cocked his head, eyeing the ever-persistent Rosie, and again tried to make light of her questioning. "My children certainly can't come to work with me. Ain't so?"

"It seems you may want to think of another solution, Jacob. I mean, generally, when you speak of Hannah your eyes light up and a smile creeps across your face. But today, you look like a sad puppy and there sure isn't any light in your eyes."

"Because I didn't get much sleep last night."

"And why is that, do you think?"

Rosie knew him almost as well as his mother ever did.

"I'm doing what's best for Hannah."

"Have you even asked her if that's what *she* wants?"

"You don't understand. You don't know her. She doesn't stop to think of herself. I'm just looking out for her." No matter how much it hurt him and his children—that was what he had to do.

As they exited the building, his surrogate aunt gave one last try.

"Well, you may think this is the best solution," Rosie appealed to him, "but I for one am not sure that having Hannah out of your life is the right one. And vice versa, if you get my drift..." Her lips curved downward before she gave him a weak wave goodbye.

Naturally, he didn't admit to Rosie that for a while he'd been thinking the same way. But after speaking to Mrs. Hochstetler, it was all too easy. Everything was falling into place. Things that were meant to be usually were that simple, weren't they?

As he got into his buggy and turned his horse toward home, he drifted off thinking about Hannah. With her, nearly everything every day just fell into place. And the feelings he'd always had for her were even greater now. It was as if their relationship was supposed to be, wasn't it?

He shook his head, working to be rid of those thoughts. He was being selfish for wanting her to be by his side. This wasn't about him. It was about her. Hannah deserved the life she'd hoped for and the chance to pursue her dream.

Besides, *Gott* knew what He was doing bringing them closer together than they'd ever been.

Jake's deep feelings for Hannah were what made him want to give up what was best for him, so he could do what was best for her.

He only hoped she would see that.

After dinner, when Jake asked if she could stay until he got the children to bed, Hannah was more than happy to oblige. He said he wanted to talk to her, and she wanted to do the same.

She'd obviously acted strangely around him following Madeline Enyart's visit the evening before. She knew Jake assumed she was angry with him for eavesdropping, but that wasn't the case at all. If she was upset with anyone, it was with herself, for feeling so conflicted.

After all, Madeline's offer should've had her thrilled and jumping at the chance to have her dream come true. Yet the idea of leaving the Burkholder household any sooner than she had to filled her with sadness. She loved them all too much to be just one more person who left them. Jake needed to know that she didn't plan to disrupt their lives anytime soon. She wanted to stay until things for him and the children—and his heart's match—were permanent.

Hopefully, Madeline would understand the timing wasn't yet right.

But if not…

Without question, I'll deal with it.

"I'm sorry that took so long." Jake came into the room, settling into the chair across from where she was seated on the sofa. She couldn't help noting how tired he looked. Even more tired than when he'd arrived home from work.

"Let me guess." She smiled. "Eli wanted you to read about horses one more time."

"Jah." She noticed her comment brought a glimmer of amusement to Jake's blue eyes just as she hoped it would. "And then—" he started.

"One more time," they chimed the words in unison.

They chuckled, both completely familiar with Eli's bedtime ploy to delay lights-out. Knowing the children as she did and even being fond of their schemes, Hannah was still smiling and feeling sure about what she wanted to say to Jake.

But the twinkle in Jake's eyes immediately faded.

Before she could speak, he leaned forward in the chair, folding his hands in his lap. "Hannah, there's something I need to say." All lightness had departed from his voice.

"Jake, if it's about last night, I'm sorry and—" She started to tell him what she'd been thinking. What she'd been feeling.

But he stopped her. "I've figured out a way that things will work out for all of us. Starting Monday, Mrs. Hochstetler is going to come watch the children. Her husband will drive her back and forth. She even said she'd start dinners, and she'll be helping me find a good nanny for the long haul. That means…" He paused. "You'll be free to form a partnership with that businesswoman."

Her entire body froze in shock. "What?"

He glanced away for a moment. Because she looked so pitiful and confused?

"Trust me, Hannah. This is what's best for you," he said adamantly. "We can't keep holding your life—you—hostage forever."

Stunned again, she squinted at him. "Have I ever said anything like that? I hope I've never seemed that way. *Jah*, I watch your children, but I also care about them. And in turn, you've given me a place to live. I've saved plenty of money and have grown a business." She shrugged. "I think it's been a *gut* arrangement for both of us."

"And now, you have the opportunity to do even more. To have your dream come true," he said more assertively than assuredly. "You need this. It's not fair to make you stay here, Hannah. And…" He stopped and took in a deep breath, letting it out slowly. "Actually, it's not fair to the *kinner*, either."

"The *kinner*?" She blinked at him, shaken. "Have I done something—"

"*Nee.*" He reached out and took her hand.

"Hannah, they've blossomed under your care. I've never seen them so happy."

She almost thought his voice quavered before he continued. "On the other hand, I think maybe they're getting too used to this—to us—to all of our times together. I'm not sure it's *gut* for them to continue that way."

Beth. That was what he was getting at and not saying it. Evidently, they were more serious than she knew and wanting to move forward. Covert or not, her matchmaking had worked again. And ready or not, the time had come. He wanted her gone.

She was trying to be brave. She was working to hold back tears. She didn't exactly know what she'd expected Jake to say, but she hadn't been prepared for this. Or the wave of grief that engulfed her completely.

"You're right. We should...whatever is best for the *kinner.*"

"It'll be what's best for you, as well."

"Oh, *jah.*" She slipped her hand from his warm grasp and stood up, working to steady herself on her feet. "I...um...should go. I'll...uh...see you... sometime," she mumbled. "The blueberries have been rinsed for tomorrow's breakfast. Don't let Clara eat too many...her stomach sometimes..." She wobbled and he caught her by the arm.

"Let me walk you home," he offered.

"You don't need to." She clenched her teeth, fighting back the tears pooling in her eyes.

"I know I don't need to, Hannah." Jake let go of her arm, then rubbed his hand briskly over his beard. A sure sign he was peeved. "You know, you want to help everyone else. And that's *wunderbaar*. But you never want help from anyone else, and that's not fair. There are people who love you and want to give to you in return. Maybe someday you'll see that."

"*Danke*, Jake," she said simply, picking up her cloak and satchel, anxious to leave.

As soon as the cool night air hit her heated face, sobs came pouring from her. As she crossed the lawn to the *dawdi haus*, Jake's mention of love kept ringing in her ears.

It was a four-letter word that made most people happy, thrilled, complete. Oh, but not her. At least not with Jake. A strangled sound erupted from deep within her. Somehow with him, love was always attached to another four-letter word— hurt. Not that he'd ever meant to hurt her. She knew that for a fact. But somehow, invariably, it always happened that way.

Chapter Sixteen

Hannah was tossing in bed the next day, glumly wondering if the birds' early-morning chirping was ever going to sound delightful to her ears again, when *Aenti* Ruth slowly rolled into the bedroom.

"I heard you stirring and thought I'd bring you some tea."

"Oh!" Hannah instantly sat up and leaned against the headboard, smoothing her disheveled hair. *"Danke, Aenti."* She took the warm mug from her hand.

"You're usually up earlier." *Aenti* Ruth gave her a worried look. "Are you sick? Abram said some people in town are getting an end-of-winter flu. You certainly don't look like yourself."

After the encounter with Jake the prior evening, she didn't quite feel like herself, either. It stood to reason that her aunt would think she was ill. Her eyes had to look red and puffy from crying so much the night before.

She'd taken a detour into the barn once she'd spied Abram's buggy in front of the *dawdi haus*. There, she'd sat pouring out her heart to the kittens and any other animal that would listen. When she finally got a hold of herself, she made her way home, giving her aunt and Abram brief hellos before heading to bed. All through the night, she couldn't stop from whimpering, burying her face in her pillow.

"I'm fine." Hannah took a sip of the tea as if that could prove what she was saying.

"No, you're not," *Aenti* Ruth retorted bluntly.

Not ready to explain, for fear she'd break down again, Hannah changed the subject. "How was your evening with Abram?"

The question caused her aunt's cheeks to immediately turn pink, which brought the slightest smile to Hannah's lips.

"*Aenti*, you're blushing. You two must have enjoyed some special time together."

Her aunt covered her mouth with her hand and giggled. "Abram asked me to marry him."

Hannah coughed, choking on the swallow of tea.

"See, I think you are getting sick." Her aunt's eyes narrowed.

"*Nee*, I'm not." She coughed again before getting her bearings. Then cleared her throat. "What did you tell Abram?"

"What do you think?" *Aenti* Ruth laughed. "I said *jah*!" she exclaimed. "Oh, Hannah, I can't tell you how happy I am!" She clapped her hands together. "I know you don't think much of Abram and me together, but—"

Hannah laid a hand on her aunt's arm. "*Aenti* Ruth, it's not that. I only want you to be happy. And I can see that you're *verra* happy with Abram, which is all that matters. I'm thrilled for you and for Abram, too," she said sincerely, knowing the pair had waited forever to find love. It was the first marriage for them both. "Really, I am."

Out of the corner of her eye, on her aunt's nightstand, she spied the "something" Abram said her aunt had left behind during their move. It was his gift of a forget-me-not plant. She should've realized then that Abram had sweet intentions.

"Honestly, we do know we're different as night and day," her aunt replied. "But Abram says we're like a magnet and a paper clip. Sometimes opposites attract each other and hold close. And we do, too." She beamed. "We have a connection… and it just works beautifully." Her aunt sighed dreamily. "Sort of like you and Jake."

Obviously, her aunt meant no harm. Even so,

the words gripped Hannah's heart. She gritted her teeth and looked away, working to hide her emotions. It seemed unimaginable that any more tears could possibly flow from her eyes. Yet they did.

"Hannah, I'm sorry. I didn't mean to upset you," her aunt said softly. She rolled closer, reaching up to stroke Hannah's hair. "What's going on, *kind*?"

"Do you think we can move back to Abram and Susan's house right away?" Hannah asked. "Can you please ask Abram if there's a vacancy?"

Aenti Ruth stared, appearing as shocked as Hannah had probably looked the night before with Jake.

"Hannah, dear, if you and Jake had a squabble, I'm sure you two can work things out. You always have." Her aunt's forehead furrowed. "I don't think we have to move."

"Oh, but I do," Hannah cried. "Jake has asked Mrs. Hochstetler to take care of the children from now on. He thinks it's what's best for me so I can be a partner in Decor to Adore. He didn't even ask what I wanted." She sniffled. "He talked about how I help everyone else, but I don't want help from anyone, and it's not fair to people who love me. And then he kicked me out of his house and life. Does that sound like love to you?"

Setting the mug on the nightstand, she grabbed

at the tissue her aunt offered. After taking a minute to blow her nose, she continued.

"And you know what, *Aenti* Ruth? This is exactly the reason why I do go around helping everyone else, whether I'm matchmaking or nannying or—"

"Taking care of an old *aenti*." Her aunt gave her an appreciative smile.

"You mean sharing life with someone important to me," Hannah corrected her. "*Aenti* Ruth, never think that I considered being with you as a job. The years we've had together have been incredibly special for me."

"Me, too, sweet Hannah. Me, too." *Aenti* Ruth patted Hannah's blanket-covered knee. They shared a look that made Hannah sigh.

"Oh, I don't know." Twisting the Kleenex in a knot, she shook her head. "Maybe Jake is right. But this is exactly why I try not to depend on anyone. Because I usually get disappointed." Or hurt. In a huge way. She left that part out.

Aenti Ruth tilted her head. "And I'm guessing you didn't speak up or tell Jake how you were feeling."

"Why would I?" Hannah rolled her eyes. "It was clear he'd already made up his mind. And, well…of course, I want to do whatever is best for him and the children, and him and Beth."

"Beth? You keep saying they're together. But

when I've seen them, I don't know how to explain it…" *Aenti* Ruth scanned the ceiling as if she'd find the right words there. Then she focused on Hannah, her eyes wide. "I know. They don't seem magnetic to me. Whereas, when I see you and Jake together, there's such a pull."

"You're starting to sound like there's a science to romance, *Aenti* Ruth." Hannah shook her head doubtfully.

"I don't know anything about science, but I do know what I see go on between you two."

"What do you mean?"

"You've always said you wanted to own your own sewing store. That's been your goal, right?"

Hannah nodded.

"So that didn't work out with Sew Easy. But now you have another answer to your dream. Jake knows all of that and loving you—"

"Uh-uh." Hannah winced.

"Okay, then. *Caring* for you the way he does, no matter what, he wants the best for you. And I've also heard you say again and again that you want the best for him." She smacked her hands together. "I don't know about you, but that sounds like a match to me. It's obvious you both want to do whatever you can to make each other happy. All except for facing your feelings for one another."

"*Jah*, well…" Hannah's shoulders slumped under the weight of disappointment.

Months ago, she'd thought if Jake could find love and make a new life for himself, that she'd also step out of her comfort zone and be willing to put her heart out there again. Now she realized what a challenge that would be, especially since her heart had already found a home with people she loved. A home that she was being vacated from.

Yet, she had to trust that *Gott* had a plan for her life and would see her through.

She had to hold on and believe that He knew what was best.

And in the meantime…

"Do you mind asking Abram about any vacancies, *Aenti* Ruth?" she asked again.

Her aunt squeezed Hannah's hand. "For you, of course I will."

Breakfast was usually the easiest meal with his children, but not so this morning. With a heavy heart, Jake had to explain that Hannah would no longer be with them.

"What do you mean she's going away?"

Clara stopped picking the blueberries off the top of the oatmeal Jake had spooned into each of the children's bowls. Licking her stained fingers, she waited for his answer.

Before he could reply, Sarah spoke up. "Is she taking a trip to see *Oncle* David and *Grossmammi*?"

"Can we go, too?" Eli asked.

While his son's eyes grew wide with excitement, Jake closed his own momentarily, whispering for help from *Gott*. Hannah meant so much to all of them that they'd certainly need His support to get them through the days ahead without her.

The night before, countless times, he'd almost gone out to the *dawdi haus* to Hannah to beg her to not go. But he had to stay the course for everyone. It was only right to do.

Taking a deep breath, he exhaled slowly, and began to explain the situation with Hannah the best way he knew how.

"You all know that Hannah enjoys sewing, *jah*?"

"Jah, Daed." Clara's blue eyes surveyed him like he was silly. "She made us Biscuit and Leo, and—"

"And my new pants and shirts." Eli nodded.

"And besides our clothes, the pretty things she's made for the house," Sarah chimed in.

"True. And because she has this gift from *Gott*, other people outside our family want her to sew things for them, too."

"Like she's doing now," Sarah insisted.

"Jah." He bit his lip, then figured he needn't keep beating around the bush. "But now there is a businesswoman who wants to form a company with Hannah. Which means Hannah needs to move back into town. So I've arranged for Mrs. Hochstetler to come watch you. You remember that nice lady, don't you?"

He'd tried to shift them from the subject of Hannah and onto the prospect of fun times with Mrs. Hochstetler. It didn't work. All three were staring at him, the two girls with tears in their eyes.

"Why can't we move to town with Hannah?" Clara wanted to know.

"Life doesn't work like that," he told her.

"Why not?" She sniffled.

"Look, *kinner*, I know this is hard for you. It is for me, as well. But I told Hannah I think she needs to do this. I think it's best for her."

"Did she think so, too?" Sarah croaked. "What did she say?"

Obviously, Hannah hadn't said anything. He hadn't given her the opportunity. "Hannah has been so good to all of us. She's given us her time, her talents and her love. Just because she isn't living in the *dawdi haus* doesn't mean she'll be completely out of our lives. We can visit her. Won't that be fun?"

His children gave him skeptical looks. He

didn't blame them. After all, how often had they gone to visit her in the past? Never. She'd always come to them.

"I know this hurts right now, but we need to think of Hannah," he continued. "Her happiness is important. Sewing and creating are special to her. Don't you all have something that's special to you? Something you like?"

"I like horses," Eli jumped in. "I'm going to ride them lots someday."

"I'm going to make puppets like Hannah does," Clara declared.

"Sarah?" He looked at his oldest, who seemed to be thinking hard. "What's special to you?"

"Hannah." Her lips quivered, and he knew she was fighting back more tears.

"I know, Sarah, I know." He got up, crossing the table to hug her.

"Can we do something special for her before she leaves, *Daed*?" his sweet daughter asked between sniffles.

"Of course we can." He gave her an extra squeeze. "After breakfast, let's think about what that could be."

"I think I already know," Sarah said, glancing around the table. "But Clara and Eli and I are gonna need you to help."

"I'm happy to," he agreed, a glimmer of hope

filling him as his daughter's expression brightened the tiniest bit.

Maybe, one day, they would all be okay after all.

Chapter Seventeen

Around noontime, sorrowfully packing up her few belongings, Hannah shook her head at herself. When she'd moved from town out to Jake's, she'd been uneasy about giving up her independence. Now she was moving back to town and regaining her independence, but she'd never felt so miserable.

She was wondering what *Gott* must think of her when a knock sounded at the front door.

At once her pulse quickened, and her mind raced. Could it be Jake, asking her to stay?

Working to control her emotions, she hurried toward the entrance, tripping over a box along the way. By the time she opened the door, there was no one to see. Nothing, except for a handmade card that had fallen from the doorframe onto the porch. Surprised, she bent to pick it up.

"What is it?" *Aenti* Ruth wheeled over, just as curious as she was.

"It's a dinner invitation for the two of us."

"To where?" her aunt asked.

"To *Kinner*'s Kitchen. Tonight, at six o'clock. The card is decorated with crayon drawings." Hannah couldn't help but smile. "I'm thinking Sarah and the twins are doing a takeoff on Kauffman's."

"How sweet!" *Aenti* Ruth grinned. "Does that mean they're doing the cooking?"

"I'm guessing so." Hannah nodded. "Plus, it says an escort will be here to pick us up at five to six."

"Abram is stopping by then to pick up some of our boxes. I'll have to pass, although it sounds like a nice evening." Her aunt chuckled.

A nice *last* evening.

That was why at five o'clock Hannah decided to stop packing. She wanted to take her time getting ready for their last meal together. Or, at least the last one until who knew when. After getting cleaned up, she brushed her hair several times before wrapping it up in a bun. And before donning her *kapp*, tried to choose a dress to wear.

She kept coming back to her violet-colored dress. Mostly because each time she wore it, Jake mentioned how nice it looked on her. Why she was even thinking about pleasing him, she didn't know. But remembering how his compliments made her feel special and especially close to him, after much pondering, that dress won out.

Ready by 5:45 p.m., she sat and waited for her mystery escort's arrival. This time she was at the door the instant she heard a knock.

When she opened the door, she gasped. "Jake!"

Since the evening was set up by the children, she'd assumed one of them would fetch her. But there he was, looking more handsome than ever, wearing her favorite blue shirt, of course, which always intensified his already too-blue eyes.

"Sorry to surprise you," he apologized. "Eli was supposed to be your escort. But he's busy arguing with the girls about which dessert you like best—applesauce, trail mix or ice cream. So you may end up with all three. He sent me in his place. I hope you don't mind."

Jake seemed nervous and her heart went out to him. Like her, he was probably hoping things wouldn't be uncomfortable between them.

"*Nee*, I don't mind having three desserts or you as my escort. I think I can manage both," she quipped.

She'd hoped her humor would put him at ease and it did. His tense jaw broke into a relaxed smile. She was determined for the evening to be a good one. They all deserved that much.

"Well, then…" Being the gentleman that he

was, he held out his arm. "Shall we head to *Kinner*'s Kitchen?"

"*Jah*, we shall."

She wrapped her arm around his without a moment's hesitation. But as they began their walk across the lawn, he took her by surprise once more.

"You look beautiful this evening." His words were just as warm as the feel of having him close.

She stopped and stared at him, wishing words like that meant something and were forevermore. But knowing they weren't, once again, she responded airily. "You've seen me in this dress plenty of times. But then, your memory isn't the best." She figured that would get a rise from him.

"*My* memory? I don't know what you're talking about." He scoffed, playfully. "I beat you at the *kinner*'s memory game almost every time. Ain't so?"

Attempting to appear thoughtful, she scratched her chin. "Not that I can recall."

His laughter filled her heart, and in good spirits, they entered *Kinner*'s Kitchen. Their mood carried over to the children, whose faces brightened the minute they saw them.

"Doesn't this look special?" Hannah let go of Jake's arm, clasping her hands together. "The table looks lovely with the candles you all arranged. And look at these place mats." She touched the edge of the one closest to her. "Did you make them yourselves?"

The three nodded. "Eli drew the horses," Sarah explained. "Clara drew dogs, and I drew the flowers and trees."

"I will keep mine forever," Hannah said truthfully, placing her hand over her heart. "The only thing is, I don't see places for you *kinner* at the table."

Clara spoke up. "That's because Sarah said we can't eat with customers."

"Workers eat in there." Eli pointed to the sitting room.

"Hmm." Hannah frowned. "Do you think we can make an exception this time?"

The twins deferred to Sarah, who beamed at the suggestion. "*Jah.* Just give us an extra minute, please," she replied, sounding so grown-up to Hannah's ears.

She and Jake took their seats at the opposite sides of the table while the children put together additional place settings. The three of them grinned proudly as they served hot dogs and baked beans, even though they confessed their *daed* had done the cooking.

"Everything looks delicious, *kinner*," Hannah complimented them. "I'm *verra* thankful for all you've done to make this a special evening."

"And I—we—can't be more thankful for you, either, Hannah." Jake's voice was low and sweet.

The children's expressions seemed to sober as they looked at her, nodding in agreement with their father.

Until Clara spoke up. "Can we hurry and tell *Gott* thank-you? I'm hungry."

Hannah didn't know whether to laugh or cry as a mixture of joy and sorrow welled up inside her. Oh, how she would miss them. Miss all of them. She looked across the table at Jake.

But still, I'm thankful, she told the Lord as they bowed their heads in prayer. *Gott* had given her a new opportunity to use her talents. It was all she'd ever hoped for.

Until these past months…until Jake and his children had become such a part of her.

Now she could barely imagine her life without them. And she wondered why she'd let her fear of being hurt keep her from being true to her heart's longings.

But time had passed, circumstances had changed and she'd missed her chance. Besides, it wasn't right, was it, to be given the answer to her dreams—and then expect *Gott* to grant her even more?

All throughout dinner, with the laughter and chatter at the table, Jake couldn't escape feeling like he'd experienced the same sort of light-hearted, joyful banter before. Even during cleanup and washing dishes—which Hannah insisted on helping with—he sensed a harmonious rhythm, reminding him of something he couldn't quite put his finger on.

It wasn't until they were playing the memory game, which he'd teased Hannah about, and the children were laughing happily, that he realized what had struck him as so familiar. It was togetherness, and the sense of family.

He'd taken those feelings for granted when he'd been growing up, but now he realized that his children might not be able to say the same thing. It was only recently that they'd come out of their shells—and they'd done that through Hannah's encouragement. He would need to remember how important moments like this were when Hannah was no longer living nearby.

He hated for the merriment to come to an end, but glancing at the clock, he knew it had to. "Guess what time it is?"

His *kinner* groaned, familiar with his nightly remark. On this night, he hated the evening coming to an end as much as they did. Especially knowing that, when they all woke up, Hannah would be leaving.

"Will you tuck us in?" He watched Sarah place a hand on Hannah's knee.

"Jah." Hannah gently cupped his daughter's cheek. "I'd love to."

As the children headed upstairs to get ready for bed, he and Hannah gathered up the game pieces.

"Are you sure you don't mind staying to say prayers with them?" he asked after a bit.

Her answer came softly. "Have I ever?"

"No, never." He'd never been so honest.

"We're all ready for bed now," Sarah called from up the stairs.

"Oll recht," Jake called back. "We're headed up. Everyone be sure to be under the covers and settled down."

As he followed Hannah up the staircase, he wondered if there would be a next time that they'd perform this ritual together. His melancholy thoughts were interrupted by Sarah's command to her siblings.

"Quiet! They're coming!" His daughter's excited and rather loud whisper was followed by sounds of rustling sheets and squeaky beds.

As he and Hannah entered the bedroom, he scratched his head. "I don't know, Hannah, it's mighty quiet in here."

"Yes, it's *verra* quiet," Hannah said seriously, playing along. "Maybe your *kinner* are already asleep."

"I think you're right. Guess we don't need to be saying prayers then, ain't so?"

"I guess not. I think I'll head home." Hannah turned, pretending to go, just as giggles erupted across the room.

"We're not asleep," Sarah assured them.

"We were trying to be quiet," Clara said.

"And *gut*," Eli added. "Sarah bossed us into it."

"I'm not bossy," Sarah protested. "That's not nice."

"But it's true, Sarah," Clara noted.

"Daed!" Sarah wailed.

As usual, the quiet had turned to chaos in a matter of seconds.

"Come on now, settle down. And no more comments about your older sister," Jake warned sternly. "Sarah is only trying to keep you two out of trouble."

As the three of them wriggled back under quilts, Sarah looked at Hannah with hopeful eyes. "Will you say that prayer from before?"

"Yeah," Eli added. "The one with the funny name."

"Eeny, meeny, miny, moe or something." Clara got in her two cents.

Hannah chuckled. "You mean *'Müde bin ich, geh zur Ruh.'"*

Hearing the name again, his children happily clasped their hands and uniformly bowed their heads. As Hannah recited the prayer, he noticed how her sweet voice created a calm peacefulness throughout the room. But as he sat at the edge of Eli's bed, he didn't hear a word she said. He was far too captivated by the sight of her, observing how the sliver of moonlight coming in the window highlighted the softness of her cheeks and enhanced the golden glow of her eyes.

So it shook him out of his reverie when he heard her ask the *kinner*, "Does anyone want a kiss?"

The children bobbed their heads simultaneously. He watched as Hannah started with Sarah, pushing back a wisp of his daughter's hair before kissing the girl's forehead.

Hannah appeared surprised when Sarah flung her arms around her neck and held tight. "I love you so much," Sarah said, looking into Hannah's eyes.

"Oh, Sarah, I love you, too." He could hear the emotion in Hannah's voice, which gave rise to his own. Finally, Hannah dabbed Sarah's nose with her finger before Sarah would let go.

Next, Clara had her arms outstretched before Hannah even crossed over to her side of the bed.

"We want to move to town with you, but *Daed* won't let us," Clara confided before quickly closing her arms around Hannah's neck and pulling her close, not waiting for Hannah's peck. It was some moments before Clara's grip loosened, and Hannah placed a soft kiss on her forehead.

"I'll be back to visit," Hannah said, bringing a smile to the girl's face.

"Promise?" Clara asked.

"*Jah*, I promise." Hannah's voice quaked and Jake knew her well enough to know she was near tears.

Yet he also knew that no matter what, she was all about putting everyone at ease. She made her way to Eli's bed and said lightly, "Last and certainly never, ever least, good night, Eli."

Bending over the bed, she started to kiss Eli's forehead when his son grabbed her around the neck and yanked her to him. His strength must've surprised her, causing her to nearly stumble off balance.

"*Danke* for being my mommy. Or like a mommy," Eli corrected himself.

"Oh, Eli…"

Jake heard a sniffle escape from Hannah before she put her arms under Eli's small shoulders and hugged him with what appeared to be the same fierceness that he was hugging her.

After a moment, Jake spoke up, his voice slightly hoarse. "It's time for sleep now, Eli. Girls."

Jake could see the tears he'd suspected brimming in Hannah's eyes the moment they got to the bottom of the stairs. His own emotions were also veering out of control.

"Hannah, I'm sorry that was so—" He couldn't think of the right word to say.

"Your *kinner* are sweet, Jake. Too precious."

"And you, Hannah…you make them even better," he said earnestly. "I don't know how to thank you. I don't know what to say."

"Then don't."

She put a finger to his lips, and he gazed hopelessly into her eyes. Before she could move away, he reached for her hand and pressed her palm to his lips. Transfixed by its softness, he turned her hand over and slowly, gently held it against the bare skin of his cheek.

Taking her other hand in his, he pulled her toward him, yearning to hold her close and never let her go.

But seeing the bewildered look in her eyes, for her sake, he knew he needed to do what was right.

He leaned his forehead against hers, still not ready to let her walk out of his life, wishing the moments could turn into an eternity.

It was too soon when she spoke.

"I… I have to go, Jake," she whispered.

"I know." Reluctantly, he let go of his grasp. "I know."

Chapter Eighteen

"It's been two weeks since Hannah moved, Jake." Beth stood in his kitchen with her hands on her hips, shaking her head. "I can't believe you haven't spoken to her even once."

"I'm sure she's been busy getting settled. Besides—" he shrugged "—what is there to say?"

"She and Ruth moved back into the Masts' house, *jah*?"

He nodded.

"Well, then, for openers, you could take that mail to her."

Beth tilted her head toward the countertop and the envelopes he'd set aside with Hannah's name on them. Many of which he assumed contained payments from clients.

Staring at those envelopes that he'd tried hard to ignore, he felt guilt stab him hard. Hannah had likely been needing that money.

Before he could say a word, Beth continued, "While you're there you should also tell Hannah you love her, Jake. It's time to do that, ain't so?" She arched a brow. "Maybe past time."

"*Jah*, well." It was his turn to shake his head. "*Danke* for stopping by to harass me, friend."

"Harass you?" She shook a finger. "You know I'm only here trying to help, Jake. And, well, also Caleb…" Her tone softened at the mention of her beau's name. "He wanted me to let you know he'll be back in town next week. Permanently." Her face flushed. "He's hoping you can find time to discuss the build-out plans of the store."

"Let him know I'm happy to," Jake replied. "And since you're giving me a piece of advice, let me give you some."

"About what?" Her hands flew back to her sides.

"You better not harass Caleb the way you do me. Not if you want him to stick around," he warned playfully. "Also, Miss Know-It-All, what you don't know is that I *am* planning to take the mail to Hannah."

He knew he shouldn't hold on to Hannah's mail or even the hope of her coming back. But her leaving had taken a toll on him, and he wasn't sure if he was ready to see her. And it wasn't only his own feelings that concerned him.

Glimpsing out the window, he eyed his children lackadaisically kicking a ball around. Since the day Hannah moved out, they had seemed somewhat listless and crankier than usual. Given time and his prayers, he knew they would adjust. But how much time was enough so that seeing Hannah again wouldn't get their hopes up?

"I may even go next Saturday," he told Beth.

She eyed him skeptically. "Hmm, I'll believe it when I see it."

Picking up her shawl, Beth turned to go, then bumped into Eli as he came flying in the back door.

"*Daed*, Hannah's here! Hannah's here!" his son shouted with a grin as wide as his face. "She's coming up the drive!"

Jake had only time to gape before Eli rushed out the door to greet her.

The day before, when Hannah discovered Clara's lion puppet mixed in with her fabric, her aunt had remarked with a smile, "The Lord moves in mysterious ways."

Additionally, *Aenti* Ruth had not been shy about stating that by giving the opportunity to return the puppet to its rightful owner, *Gott* had provided a chance for Hannah to share her feelings with Jake, as well.

But as soon as Hannah pulled in Jake's driveway and saw Beth's buggy, she was reminded of what she'd known all along—her aunt's thinking didn't appear in line with their heavenly Father's. And as much as she'd hoped otherwise, if she didn't want to be totally estranged from the Burkholder household, she would have to be at peace with that.

"Hannah! Hannah!"

The children's delighted squeals immediately drowned out any reservations she'd had about stopping by. At once, her heart warmed, and the world felt like it had set itself right again. At least temporarily.

She couldn't halt her speckled horse, hitch it to a post and grab her tote from the buggy quickly enough so she could run to them.

"How I've missed you!" She pulled the three *kinner* into a tight embrace. "So, so much!"

"We've missed you, too," Sarah murmured, nestling in.

"Are you staying for supper?" Eli was the first to break free from her hug.

"We can make grilled cheese like you used to make us," Clara offered.

Gazing at their earnest faces just about broke her heart. "Some other time that would be *wunderbaar*." Preferably when she'd been invited by their father. "But today I wanted to bring you something."

"Besides you?" Sarah questioned.

"Jah." She caressed the sweet girl's *kapp* before patting the tote hanging at her side.

Eli noticed and, in a flash, stuck his nose into her satchel. "It's a white bag." He looked up at her. "Is it chocolate-covered pretzels?"

"With sprinkles?" Clara stepped closer for a look.

"Yes, with sprinkles." Hannah grinned.

"Can we go inside and eat them? I don't want the kitties to get them."

"Neither does Leo." Hannah pulled the puppet from her tote.

"Leo!" Clara shouted. "He's alive!" She clapped her hands. "I need to show *Daed*."

With Leo in her grasp, Clara took off running into the house. Her sister and brother hurried behind her. Meanwhile, as much as Hannah longed to see Jake again, and hopefully his smiling eyes, all at once her heart pounded. Her legs felt locked in place.

You must get over this. Over him, she scolded herself. *If you want to keep these people in your life, you have to take that step.*

Forcing herself to move, she plodded toward the house. The short distance to Jake's door felt like a thousand miles.

Hopefully, it would get easier. Hopefully, with just one step at a time.

* * *

It seemed strange to Jake to be courteously holding the back door open for Hannah. In past months, he'd become happily accustomed to her comings and goings being one of the very best parts of his everyday life.

Their greeting was polite but strained, which bothered him, as well. Forever and a day, they'd enjoyed an easygoing connection with each other.

But while some things changed, Jake thought, some things didn't. Like the way a light, pleasant vanilla scent always trailed behind her, teasing his senses, making her seem so familiar to him. And how her very presence could fill every empty corner of his house. Not to mention the effect she had on his children, bringing out their smiles and lifting their hearts. And his, too.

"*Danke* for bringing Leo back." He chose a safe subject.

"I had to. The little lion was missing his keeper."

She looked from him to Clara, who was busy reintroducing Leo to his habitat. Then he saw her turn to Beth.

"How are you, my friend?" She hugged Beth. "I've been meaning to drop by Kauffman's and visit. I've missed you."

"I miss you, too." Beth smiled. "When can we get together?"

"Well, my schedule is flex—" Hannah started.

Before she could finish, his son tugged on her sleeve.

"May we eat the pretzels now?" Eli asked.

"Oh, of course. How silly of me." Hannah chuckled. "I only meant to drop those off and be on my way."

"So soon?" Beth questioned Hannah. "I have to run to work. Why don't you stay and visit?"

"Oh…well…no." Hannah shook her head. "I mean, I think my buggy is probably blocking yours anyway. I was so excited about bringing Leo back home and then rushing to greet the children."

Jake could tell Hannah was uncomfortable and most likely couldn't wait to leave. He wished she'd see in his eyes how much he wanted her to stay.

As she laid out the treats from her satchel, Beth caught his attention, nodding toward his countertop.

"You can't go yet," he said a little too forcefully.

"I can't? Why not?"

"Because…because I have something that belongs to you."

"You do?" She appeared even more curious.

"*Jah. Jah*, I do."

He wished he could say it was his heart that belonged to her, but he couldn't imagine what she would think of that. Instead, stepping toward the kitchen counter, he picked up her mail and handed it to her.

"Thank you, Ja—"

Before Hannah could finish his name, an envelope trickled to the floor. As they both stooped to reach for it, the warmth of her hand touching his caught him off guard.

"Sorry to be so clumsy," he uttered. But that wasn't true at all. The moment his eyes locked with hers it made him wish he'd dropped every piece of mail.

"You're fine," she said bashfully as they both stood up together. And unless he was fooling himself, he didn't seem to be the only one who felt something. Hannah appeared shaken as her cheeks turned a dusty rose.

"Daed." Sarah touched his arm. "May I go down to the mailbox and see if Hannah got anything else?"

"Uh, *jah*, sure." He nodded. "Just be careful, hear?"

Sarah waved in response and skipped out the door.

In the meantime, while the women resumed their conversation and discussions about Ruth and Abram's upcoming wedding, he settled the twins at the table with their treats.

While everyone appeared to be doing just fine,

ten minutes later a sick feeling crept into the pit of his stomach.

What was taking Sarah so long?

Apparently, Hannah was wondering the same thing. Interrupting Beth, she turned to him, her forehead creased with worry.

"Shouldn't Sarah be back by now?" she asked anxiously.

The door slammed behind them as they flew outside, leaving the twins with Beth.

Without a sign of Sarah anywhere, feelings of dread surged through him again and again.

"Sarah! Sarah!" He called down the driveway. He yelled her name in every direction. But no answer came.

"Please, Sarah, say something." Hannah tried a softer approach. "Anything, sweet *maedel*. Anything," she urged, turning left and right and back again.

Still, silence filled the air, except for Hannah choking on a sob. "Oh, Jake," she clutched his arm. "Where is she? Where's our girl?"

Panicked beyond belief, they rushed toward the road, calling Sarah's name. The driveway never seemed so long and endless. It seemed forever before they reached its bottom.

And there she was. His Sarah, stricken down and lying motionless in the gulley. Hurled nearly ten feet from the mailbox, blood trickled down her forehead. Envelopes lay scattered on the grass and over the road.

"Oh, *Gott* in Heaven, help us! Please!" he moaned, breaking into sobs. Bending down, he held his oldest *dochder* close, rocking her limp, unconscious body in his arms.

"No! No! No!" He heard Hannah scream defiantly as if declaring what he was fearing—that Sarah couldn't be close to death.

"No!" she shouted again. Then she rushed across the road to the phone shanty.

Chapter Nineteen

❧

"Mr. and Mrs. Burkholder?"

Like Jake, Hannah had been holding her breath and praying her heart out for the past hour as they sat side by side in the hospital's trauma waiting room. Fearful of what the scans and X-rays would yield regarding Sarah's condition, Hannah found her anxiety intensified by the sound of the doctor's voice as she and Jake stood up to hear the results.

"Hannah is not my wife," Jake clarified. "She is my children's nanny."

"*Was* his children's nanny," Hannah further explained. "Is there any news?"

Looking surprised, the physician who had introduced herself earlier as Dr. Asbury glanced between them before she spoke. "I'm sorry. I had just assumed when I first saw you both..." She shook her head as if to clear it. "Anyway, as I was about to say, considering the circumstances, I'm happy to report that I have good news for you."

"You do?" Jake's voice croaked.

"I'm not saying that Sarah is totally out of the woods." The *doktah* held up her hand. "She has definitely suffered a mild concussion. But there is no indication of any brain damage or significant trauma to her skull. Also, test results indicate Sarah has a stable tibia fibula fracture of her right leg. It can be painful but will not require surgery. She will need to see an orthopedic doctor so that can be further taken care of."

Hannah let out a sigh of relief as heavy as Jake's, while the doctor continued giving care instructions for the concussion as well as providing orthopedic referrals. Dr. Asbury also suggested Sarah stay at the hospital under their care for a few hours longer until she completely stabilized from the accident.

"Fortunately, Sarah wasn't ejected onto the road," Dr. Asbury continued. "She was thrown onto the grass, and with spring nearly here the ground is softer. Of course, none of us know how fast the hit-and-run driver was going, but considering everything, this could've turned out—well, let's just say much worse."

"Jah." Jake voice quaked as he bowed his head. "I can't even—"

For the first time since they'd arrived at the

hospital, Jake's shoulders began to shake uncontrollably. He placed his hand over his mouth and beard as if he could possibly hide his emotions.

"I understand," Dr. Asbury said. "I have young children, too." She paused momentarily. "It will still be a while before they bring Sarah back into her room. You're welcome to wait here or step away for coffee or something."

"We'll wait," Hannah spoke up for them both.

Dr. Asbury smiled slightly. "Again, I totally understand." She started to go, then stopped and turned. "I'll be going off duty soon, but another doctor will be checking in with you after a bit. My best to all of you."

"Danke," Hannah replied once more since Jake still appeared too overwhelmed to speak. "Thank you very much."

As soon as Dr. Asbury left, Hannah felt the tightness in her chest loosen. Tears began to flow freely down her cheeks as wave after wave of emotion washed over her. Wanting so badly to comfort Jake. Wanting also to celebrate with him. Wishing to be close and feel the reassuring warmth of him.

Taking a bold step forward, she couldn't resist throwing her arms around his neck.

"Oh, Jake. Sarah's going to be all right." She gazed into his eyes, their bright blue color dimmed by his tears—and her own. "Praise *Gott* for answering our prayers!"

Without a moment's hesitation, he placed his arms around her waist and pulled her near to him. Right where her heart desired to be. "I'm very thankful. I am. It's just…for such a little one…" His voice faltered. "She's been through so much, Hannah…so *verra* much."

"I know, Jake, I know." She freed a hand to wipe at his tears and took a moment to dab her own. "But you're a wonderful father," she said sincerely, clasping her hands around his broad shoulders once more. "Your children know you're there for them. They know you always will be."

"I don't know what I'd do if anything happened to her, Hannah." His expression turned even more bewildered. "All these years I've loved Sarah like she's my own—like my very own daughter."

Hannah froze in his arms, his words swirling about her head.

Ever so slowly, she released her hands. As he eased his arms from around her waist, she took a step back.

"Wh-what?" She gasped.

"I've been wanting to tell you, but when you said you didn't want to know anything more about my marriage to Lily, I decided to keep it to myself. And maybe this isn't the right time…" He shook his head, glancing around the room before settling his eyes on her again. "But I don't know if there is a time that's right. I really don't." He held out his hands imploringly. "All I know is that I don't want any more secrets between us. You mean too much to me, Hannah, and to my children. You're closer to us than anyone on this earth."

She started to say she was shocked but couldn't. Not if she was being honest. After all, besides Sarah's blue eyes, she'd always wondered why the child looked so different from Lily and Jake. And for the longest time, ever since Lily and Jake married, hadn't she felt like Lily was hiding something from her? Apparently, it hadn't been just a feeling.

"It was the *Englisch* boy, wasn't it?" she blurted. "The boy from Kentucky who was in Sugarcreek visiting his cousin that summer?"

Until now, Hannah had forgotten how many times that summer she'd come home at curfew only to find the bed next to hers—Lily's—empty. And how many times, before she left to take care of her aunt in Indiana, had she made up excuses for Lily when Noah and Rachel Keim asked about their daughter's whereabouts?

"I know the person Lily was with was an *Englischer* and he was from out of state. But I didn't ask many questions back then," Jake confessed. "Lily was a mess about it all. I think a part of her felt ashamed. But looking back, I think a greater part of her was devastated when that boy left. I think she truly loved him." He paused. "And then, too, the Keim household became such a wreck."

"Noah's health took a turn for the worse around then, didn't it?" Hannah remembered that when she'd returned to Sugarcreek, her friends' upcoming wedding wasn't the only thing to be sad about. That was when she had also learned about Noah's lung cancer.

Jake nodded. "But he was never too ill to remind Lily that you were the perfect daughter and not her."

"Oh, no," Hannah moaned. "I wish Lily had shared this with me," she said. "I wish I could've helped in some way." Instead of praying selfishly for herself and her hurting heart back then, she could've been praying for her friend. "You're a good, caring person, Jake."

"No, I'm a blessed person." He dismissed her compliment. "When I think about Sarah's real father, I feel sorry for him. He's never known about her existence. He'll never know what a sweet, good-hearted child she is," he said quietly. "I'm so thankful she's in my life."

"And as far as Lily…" He sighed. "Her depression and despondency began even before Sarah was born. I thought trying to have another child might make us more of a family. But when the twins came along, things only got worse. Lily kept saying I should have a better life. But I thought I had a good one with children I loved." He sighed heavily. "And then when she started with the painkillers…"

Jake literally shuddered. Hannah placed a hand on his arm. "I'm sorry, Jake."

"I can't tell you how tired I am of letting everyone down." With a sigh, he continued, "First, I wasn't the man Lily needed me to be. Then, I betrayed your trust by not being honest with you." Though he was still visibly shaken, he looked her directly in the eye. "I know this isn't the best moment to speak of the past, but I couldn't wait any longer, Hannah. It was high time I told you."

Right then, a medical assistant wheeled Sarah's bed into the room. As soon as the young man locked the bed into place, she and Jake quietly stepped toward it.

Sarah's eyes were closed, and her body lay still. Hannah noticed that even with all her injuries, the child's face appeared peaceful.

With her eyes welling up again at the sight of this precious child, she slipped her arm through Jake's, leaning her head against his shoulder.

"Jake, what you're saying isn't true," she whispered to him. "Not true at all. You haven't let anyone down. Most of all not your children and not this sweet *maedel*. You could've disowned her. You could've made her feel less than. But instead you chose to love her and hold her close. Like you said, you love her like your daughter."

She smiled up at him and was glad to see some of the worrisome shadows disappearing from his face. Since she couldn't tell him all she wanted to, namely, that he was the best of men and the one her heart adored, she hoped what she had said would somehow bring him peace.

And at that moment, she decided to make her own peace with the past. She needed to stop asking herself and *Gott* why she and Jake never got a chance at love when they were young. Instead, she needed to remind herself that however much Jake loved Lily, he took on Lily's problem and made it his own. Despite all that had happened through the years, he never wavered from thinking of Sarah as a special gift and a blessing.

In truth, Hannah knew exactly what he meant. The time she spent as the children's nanny and now even on the periphery of their lives, was a gift she couldn't deny. And maybe that was what all of this was about after all—being given a blessing she'd be eternally thankful for.

Sarah roused just long enough to give both him and Hannah a weak smile. After that, Jake noticed Hannah appeared more comfortable about leaving.

"I need to go tell Beth and the twins the good news."

"Hannah, I… I can't thank you enough…" He couldn't believe the way his voice quivered, saying those words out loud.

Hannah being Hannah, she pretended not to notice. "I'll see you later, then." She smiled sweetly.

Though he wanted to do much more than merely squeeze her hand gratefully before she departed, unfortunately, that was all he had the nerve for.

Shutting the hospital room door behind her and silencing the hallway noise, he took another long look at his daughter. When at last he knew Sarah was resting soundly, he sank into the bedside chair. He was exhausted and extremely relieved.

Closing his eyes, he couldn't stop his mind from continually praising the Creator who had delivered his little girl from harm. He also thanked *Gott* repeatedly for Hannah's presence through it all and for the chance to bare his secrets with her. Because of the way he cared so much for her, setting things right lightened his heart. He'd been set free.

As he relaxed even more, little by little his thoughts drifted. He began to doze off to sleep when the door to the room opened, startling him. Opening his eyes, he expected to see a nurse or physician. He was shocked to see neither.

"David?" Completely taken aback by his former brother-in-law's appearance, he shook his head in disbelief. "Am I dreaming?"

For as long as Jake could remember, David had been a brash, somewhat arrogant person. Today, however, David all but tiptoed into the room, appearing sheepish.

"No, you're not," David replied. "Though I'm sure you might think so. It's been a while, hasn't it?"

"Nearly two years." Jake nodded.

"Jah." David tugged self-consciously at his straggly beard. "I stopped by your house to let you know I finally closed on my parents' property. You'll be getting new neighbors soon," he reported. "But then Beth told me all about Sarah's accident. I had to come right away and find out how she's doing."

It seemed strange that after all this time, David would be concerned about his niece. He'd hardly reached out to Jake in past years, and he certainly hadn't been good about replying to the few letters Jake had sent. Yet instead of reminding David of that, Jake chose to ignore those things. David had gone out of his way to come, so he gladly shared everything about Sarah's condition.

"She'll be all right, then?" David asked as he stood by her bed, staring.

"*Jah*, she will."

"She's grown up a lot."

"You have no idea." Jake chuckled fondly.

With that, David turned to face him. "Jake, I—" he started. "Is Hannah still here?"

"No, you just missed her." Jake frowned. "Why?"

"I saw her in town a while ago, and I wanted to say something." David rubbed his hands together nervously. "Actually, I want to tell you both. I can't live with myself any longer if I don't speak up and get this out."

"I know what you're going to say," Jake interrupted. "I know you blame me for Lily's death. I'm sure that's why you've kept your distance." He held out his arms in surrender. "Trust me, David, I have issues with myself. I've been begging for *Gott*'s forgiveness. I also pray you and your *mamm* will forgive me…someday."

"Forgive you?" David scoffed. "You're not the one to blame for Lily's death. I am. It's me." He thumped his fist against his own chest. "It's my lies that took my sister's life. It's my selfishness that kept you and Hannah apart."

Chapter Twenty

Two weeks later

No winter lasts forever. No spring skips its turn.

As Jake hitched his best horse to the family buggy, he could almost hear his mother's voice echoing those words in his ear. When he was a young *buwe*, it was a saying she frequently delighted in sharing.

He was never sure where she'd heard the adage. He'd never cared to ask. In fact, any truths buried in those words were lost to him back then. He was far too busy being a footloose youngster, lighthearted and carefree.

"But I sure understand now, *Mamm*," he said wistfully as he stroked his horse's mane.

Even though twittering birds filled the air with their musical tribute to spring, and the gray color of the landscape was quickly fading, making way for renewing shades of green, he knew more than ever his mother hadn't been lecturing about the change of seasons. Rather, she'd wanted to give him a way to visualize *Gott*'s miraculous display of hope. Something he could hold on to throughout the seasons of his life.

But that sentiment was only helpful, he now realized, if a person was willing to let go of the past. To move forward. And not allow the winter to drag on.

Finally, he was willing—and didn't want to waste any more time.

"*Daed*, I made sure the twins got the bags." Sarah interrupted his thoughts.

It had only been two weeks since she'd left the hospital. Yet even with her cast and crutches, Sarah was the first at his side.

"*Danke* for seeing to that, *dochder*." He squeezed her shoulder lovingly, then looked over her head. Clara was trudging down the walk with her gift bag in tow. Eli had his hands full, too, and was last in line.

"Did you shut the door, Eli?" Jake asked though he could clearly see the answer with his own eyes.

"Uh..." Eli dropped his bag and went running back to the house to close up.

Meanwhile, Jake helped Sarah get settled in the front of the buggy, with her crutches. Then noticed Clara in the back seat, hugging her bag in her lap.

Both girls seemed more serious than usual. He supposed that had much to do with the weighty conversations he'd had with his children throughout the week. But he felt it was only right to let them know what he intended to do. When they agreed it was what they wanted, as well, they all began making plans as to how to go about it.

Still, he made sure to warn them that sometimes things don't turn out as one might wish. However, he hoped and prayed that they remembered the other bit of advice he'd passed on—that whenever they felt *Gott* was leading their hearts in a direction, they shouldn't be afraid to give that direction a try.

After Eli jumped into the buggy with his bag, it was time to go. Jake's hands felt sweaty as he picked up the reins. He wondered if his children were nervous, too.

As he drove past his new mailbox and turned onto the road, he couldn't help but think how Sarah's accident had changed people's perspectives. Even his own. Time, relationships and truth had become more precious. It had been a day of owning up. And though it distressed him to think that Sarah's trauma was the catalyst, he had to believe that was how *Gott* had it planned all along.

That day at the hospital, Hannah had been surprised but understanding when he'd opened up and shared his long-held secret. But even more shocking was David's unprompted visit and confession.

David had revealed that he had come up with his plan to unite Lily and Jake for his own selfish reasons. He didn't want to be stuck in Sugarcreek taking care of an ailing father and a single, pregnant sister. He was smitten with a girl named Mary who was moving to Middlefield, and he wanted to follow her there. That was why David had lied and lied again.

David had given Lily his word that he'd gone to Kentucky and confronted the *Englisch* boy she cared so deeply for about her pregnancy, only to have a door shut in his face. The truth was David never made the trip at all. Regardless of his sister's wants, he'd been afraid that if Lily stepped outside her faith, it would cause a family uproar and his father's ill health would worsen rapidly.

And Jake had taken David at his word back then, too. He believed that David really had heard from a reliable person that Hannah had found her true love in Indiana. And Jake had been so crushed he hadn't even checked out David's so-called source. But then, as David admitted, that was what he'd counted on.

Then, David had sinfully used *Gott*'s name to conclude his deceitful scheme, telling Jake it was His plan that Jake should be free to help Lily. Again, Jake had taken that to heart, and Lily had believed it, too. After all, they were young. They were hurting. They wanted to find something— someone—to hold on to. Yet things never got better for them as a couple or for him as a widower. Not until now, his heart lifted at the thought— now that he had accepted *Gott*'s healing grace.

"Are we almost there, *Daed*?" Eli spoke up.

"We're getting close," Jake replied. Glancing at his twins, he saw their small hands were pressed together, in prayer.

He'd also had plenty to pray about lately. Besides Sarah's healing and his family's future, he'd been praying for David, too. He'd done everything he could to convince David to forgive himself. From experience, he knew David's confession alone would be a place to start. They'd promised to pray for each other and meet again soon. For that, Jake was glad.

Besides, Jake couldn't totally blame David for how he'd lost Hannah all those years ago. Jake had never even tried to go after her. Despite his hurting, he'd truly believed she was happy. Unwilling to risk more injury to his pride, he'd left matters at that.

And then, there he was, doing the same thing only weeks ago. Letting the love of his life go, almost forcing her to leave. He'd taken a blessing that *Gott* had wanted to give him and twisted it into something else, not thinking he was worthy enough to receive it.

Now, he prayed for *Gott* to be gracious and give him one more chance. A chance to begin a new season in his family's life.

He was ready. His children were, too.

"Keep praying, *kinner*," he said. "We're almost there."

"They're here!"

Aenti Ruth turned from the living room window, appearing mighty happy to give Hannah the news. That was after Hannah had noticed her aunt peeking outside at least a dozen times in the past hour.

"Who is here?" Hannah came close, looking over her aunt's shoulders.

"Jake and his *kinner*."

Her pulse quickened as she watched Jake and the children exit their buggy. She couldn't suppress her smile. Ever since the day she and Jake had spent at the hospital being together through all the bad and, thankfully, all the good, she hadn't been able to stop thinking of him.

"Did you know they were coming?"

Her aunt's hand flew to her chest. "How would I know?"

Hannah tilted her head. "Because even though

you say you only have eyes for your fiancé, you seem to know an awful lot about everyone else's comings and goings."

"You say that because you're still wondering why Beth and Caleb's engagement wasn't a surprise to me like it was to you, my matchmaking niece. And I keep telling you it's because—"

"I know. You sensed their magnetic pull a while ago."

"And I was right." Her aunt preened. "Now go greet your visitors."

"They probably want to see you, too, *Aenti* Ruth."

"And they will in a bit." Her aunt began rolling her wheelchair toward the kitchen. "Right now, I promised Abram I'd make a sandwich for him."

"But he just ate breakfast." Her aunt was truly the worst at making up excuses.

"Niece, would you please get out there? Now?" Her aunt shooed her.

Truth be told, Hannah couldn't wait to get her arms around Jake's children. She'd also been missing them in the worst way. Even with plenty of work and clients, life felt empty without them. Day after day, she thought about paying them a visit. But once she knew Sarah was recovering well and Mrs. Hochstetler was having no problems watching them, she'd thought she should back off.

Until now. Her heart raced as she sprinted out the door.

"It's so *gut* to see you," she gushed. "So *verra gut*."

Even on crutches, Sarah made it to the top of the wraparound porch easily via the ramp. Hannah opened her arms wide as Jake's eldest came and laid her head on her shoulder. Never ones to be outdone, the twins ran up the stairs, dropped their bags by the railing, then raced to wrap their arms around her waist. The warmth of the three of them, the joy of seeing them, quickly brought a rush of misty tears to her eyes.

"I've missed you so much." She kissed the tops of their heads. "So much." She squeezed them tight until she heard a sound she knew quite well. It was Jake clearing his throat, playfully.

"Ahem."

Looking up from the children, she saw Jake's blue eyes twinkling as he stood before her. He was also holding his hands behind his back, looking almost like he was hiding something from her. "And what about me?" His golden brows arched. "Have you missed me, too… I hope?"

His voice was both teasing and alluring, nearly seizing the breath from her. She was glad the children's embrace steadied her trembling legs.

"Now that you mention it," she jested, "I suppose I have missed you, as well."

"We've missed you," Sarah spoke up, diverting their conversation. "Have you been busy sewing?" she asked sweetly.

"As a matter of fact, I have."

Jake leaned forward, suddenly looking more serious. "How are things going with the Decor to Admire lady?"

The children gazed up at her, as well. It surprised her that they appeared intent on listening.

"You mean Decor to Adore?" She smiled. "Well, it's a funny thing," she began to explain. "One morning while I was praying, I kept getting the sense that I should stay on my own as Hannah Miller Designs. I mean, I've been blessed to build a *gut* following. And the same question kept running through my mind—did I really want to be partners with someone I didn't know?"

"That doesn't sound funny to me," Jake countered.

"Because that's not the funny part," she mused, recalling *Gott*'s timing. "That very afternoon Madeline stopped by to tell me she was pulling out of Sugarcreek and may even lose her Columbus studio. Evidently, her husband has a gambling addiction. Sadly, because of that, they've recently lost a lot of money."

"That's awful." Jake frowned. "Well, then..." Jake cleared his throat again. This time he seemed more nervous than playful. "We, uh, came by today because we also have a sort of business proposal for you," he said, as a few beads of perspiration began dotting his forehead. "Don't we, *kinner*?"

"A what, *Daed*?" Clara asked, and Eli blinked.

"Just nod your heads yes," Sarah quietly instructed her siblings.

Confused, Hannah shrugged. "I'm not sure what you mean."

"We're hoping you'll change the name of your business," Jake stated.

She lifted her brow questioningly. "You think there's a better name?"

"We do." Jake nodded. "If you would, we'd be mighty happy if you'd choose to call your business Hannah *Burkholder* Designs. And before you decide…" He paused briefly. "If you will change your name and want to continue to live in town, that's fine. We'll pack up and move. Or if you want to live out in the country, that's fine, too. We want to be with you wherever you want to be, Hannah."

Hannah laughed nervously. Was she hearing right? "Jake, are you saying—" She searched his eyes.

"Not just me. We." His smile widened as he took one arm from behind his back, extending it toward the children.

As if on cue, Sarah raised a crutch and gently

poked her brother's leg. "Now," she whispered. "It's time."

As Sarah stepped from Hannah's arms, the twins also moved quickly. Picking up their totes, the two rushed back to Hannah's side.

Eli was the first to open his bag. "We want to give you our hearts," he said in a sweet, sincere voice as he handed Hannah fistfuls of paper hearts.

"All of them," Clara chimed in. Removing more cutout hearts from her bag, she tossed them gently toward Hannah like fairy dust.

"Every one," Sarah said with a hopeful smile as she leaned on her crutches, making a heart shape with her thumbs and index fingers.

As pink, red, white and purple hearts overflowed from Hannah's hands and carpeted the porch, her heart overflowed, too. Tears trickled down her cheeks.

"Oh, children. Oh, Jake." She looked up at him, still not sure what to say.

"Hannah." He answered the question in her eyes. "We don't want to live without you, and we hope you feel the same. And, uh…" At last he brought both hands out from behind his back. In one of them was a sizable bouquet. "I wanted to give you these." He presented the flowers to her.

"They're beautiful, Jake." She sniffed at the roses. "I've never seen anything so pretty."

"I have." His gaze was as soft as a caress, sending a warm sensation tingling up her neck. "It seems kind of silly now, but I got these flowers so I could be a matchmaker myself." He pointed to the bouquet. "The yellow roses remind me of your golden eyes that I love—whether they're lighting up with your smile or eyeing me like I'm out of my mind when I do something silly."

She laughed. "I'm sorry that I do that."

"*Nee.* I generally deserve it." He winked. "The pink roses are reminders of your rosy cheeks."

Hannah blushed at that.

Jake continued. "The red roses are a symbol of all the love that I have in my heart for you. And it's a lot. So much."

"You're going to make me cry again."

"Ah, but wait." He held up a finger. "The white hydrangeas are there because I know you like them."

"Really? You remember that day at Klinger's Farm when we sat on the stone wall and these flowers were everywhere?" She gently touched the fragile petals.

"The day we first kissed?" He smiled sweetly. "How could I forget?" He took her free hand in his. "I have loved you for so many years. There's so much I want to tell you, and I will. But right now, I need to know—will you be my match, Hannah? *Our* match? Will you marry me?"

She glanced at their sweet faces, one after another, and couldn't believe the blessing she'd been given. Every day she would be able to see them. Every day she would be able to love them close up, not from far away.

"*Jah*, oh, yes!" She gazed at them with all the love in her heart. "I love you. All of you. I can't wait to marry you."

As she waved her bouquet like a magic wand, the twins began skipping around the porch, tossing the paper hearts into the air. Sarah stood giggling at the scene.

"What's all the uproar?" *Aenti* Ruth peeked out the door.

"We're getting married," Eli shouted. "We're going to have a *mamm*!"

"That sounds like something to celebrate," *Aenti* Ruth said. "You *kinner* need to come inside right now for a treat." Her aunt winked at her. Right then, Hannah knew her aunt had known about Jake's proposal all along.

The moment the children hurried indoors, Jake took the flowers from her hands, pulling her close.

"This may be the only alone time we have." He gazed at her longingly. "So I need to ask— Hannah, may I kiss you?" He rubbed his thumb gently along her cheek.

"Yes, Jake," she said. "*Jah*, please do."

As his lips met hers, she realized this kiss felt nothing like their first one. There was no hesitation this time, no doubt. The love she felt in her heart was like nothing she could've ever imagined.

Suddenly the door opened again. Clara ran out and tugged on Jake's pant leg and her skirt.

"You need to come in." Her blue eyes were wide. "There's raspberry scones."

As Clara grabbed each of their hands and led the way, Hannah looked over at her husband-to-be. She could feel her heart swell all over again.

"Ready to go inside, Jake?"

"Yes, indeed."

His adoring eyes smiled at her in the most affectionate way, letting her know there was a perfect time for absolutely everything…even for love.

* * * * *

Dear Reader,

I can't tell you how thankful and thrilled I am to have my first publication with Love Inspired. It's been a dream of mine for many years. I'm thankful to you, as well, for being a part of that dream come true.

I enjoyed writing the scenes with Hannah and Jake and his children the most. I guess it reminded me of our kids' antics when they were younger, and now the happy times we enjoy with our grandchildren. But Hannah and Jake would've never had the chance for a future together if they hadn't finally let go of all that held them to the past. For Hannah, that meant getting over the fear of being hurt again. For Jake, it meant finally forgiving himself for mistakes he'd made.

I don't know about you, but I've been in their shoes before. But I've also learned, time and again, that when I commit to trusting God, He certainly knows what's best for me far better than I do. Imagine that!

In the coming year, I wish you the best of health, happiness and all good things, plus plenty of quiet time to relax and read. Also, I'd love to hear from you at my website cathyliggett.com or on Facebook. And please let me know if you'd like to receive a bookmark/scripture card. I'd be happy to send you one!

Blessings now and always,
Cathy Liggett

Get 4 FREE REWARDS!

We'll send you 2 FREE Books plus 2 FREE Mystery Gifts.

Love Inspired books feature uplifting stories where faith helps guide you through life's challenges and discover the promise of a new beginning.

FREE Value Over **$20**

YES! Please send me 2 FREE Love Inspired Romance novels and my 2 FREE mystery gifts (gifts are worth about $10 retail). After receiving them, if I don't wish to receive any more books, I can return the shipping statement marked "cancel." If I don't cancel, I will receive 6 brand-new novels every month and be billed just $5.24 each for the regular-print edition or $5.99 each for the larger-print edition in the U.S., or $5.74 each for the regular-print edition or $6.24 each for the larger-print edition in Canada. That's a savings of at least 13% off the cover price. It's quite a bargain! Shipping and handling is just 50¢ per book in the U.S. and $1.25 per book in Canada.* I understand that accepting the 2 free books and gifts places me under no obligation to buy anything. I can always return a shipment and cancel at any time. The free books and gifts are mine to keep no matter what I decide.

Choose one: ☐ **Love Inspired Romance Regular-Print** (105/305 IDN GNWC) ☐ **Love Inspired Romance Larger-Print** (122/322 IDN GNWC)

Name (please print)

Address   Apt. #

City   State/Province   Zip/Postal Code

Email: Please check this box ☐ if you would like to receive newsletters and promotional emails from Harlequin Enterprises ULC and its affiliates. You can unsubscribe anytime.

Mail to the Harlequin Reader Service:
IN U.S.A.: P.O. Box 1341, Buffalo, NY 14240-8531
IN CANADA: P.O. Box 603, Fort Erie, Ontario L2A 5X3

Want to try 2 free books from another series! Call 1-800-873-8635 or visit www.ReaderService.com.

Visit
ReaderService.com
Today!

As a valued member of the Harlequin Reader Service, you'll find these benefits and more at ReaderService.com:

- Try 2 free books from any series
- Access risk-free special offers
- View your account history & manage payments
- Browse the latest Bonus Bucks catalog

Don't miss out!

If you want to stay up-to-date on the latest at the Harlequin Reader Service and enjoy more content, make sure you've signed up for our monthly News & Notes email newsletter. Sign up online at ReaderService.com or by calling Customer Service at 1-800-873-8635.